Please Pass Grandma's Leg

AKA: The Case of the Sacked Potatoes

To Drake,
Best Wishes,
Christina Petrell Kalberig

Other Books by Christine Petrell Kallevig

Carry Me Home Cuyahoga: A Children's Historical Novel

Fold-Along Stories: Quick and Easy Origami Tales For Beginners

Holiday Folding Stories: Storytelling and Origami Together For Holiday Fun

Bible Folding Stories: Old Testament Stories and Paperfolding Together As One

All About Pockets: Storytime Activities For Early Childhood

Folding Stories: Storytelling and Origami Together As One

Please Pass Grandma's Leg

AKA: The Case of the Sacked Potatoes

Christine Petrell Kallevig

International

P. O. Box 470505, Cleveland, Ohio 44147

Storytime Ink International
P. O. Box 470505
Cleveland, OH 44147-0505
Email: storytimeink@att.net
Telephone: 440-838-4881

ISBN 0-9628769-3-3

Library of Congress Control Number: 2003096756

Printed in The United States of America
10987654321

Acknowledgments
Many thanks to Michele Ariano at the Juvenile Diabetes Research Foundation for providing the information about Juvenile Diabetes printed on page 123.

Author's Note

When I was a teenager, I came home from school one afternoon and found my grandmother showing her artificial leg to a group of my sister's friends. As she passed it around, she demonstrated how it was attached, explained the amputation process, and encouraged the enthralled children to be careful so that this didn't happen to them.

"But if you do lose a leg, it's not the end of the world," she proclaimed. "Isn't my new one nice?"

Like the grandmother portrayed in this book, mine was also diabetic. Catching her showing off her leg that sunny afternoon has remained a profound and poignant memory all these years later.

I dedicate this book to her in recognition of her courage, spunk, and generosity. I was blessed to know you, Grandma. Thank you for our short time together. I'll love you always.

For Eva May Ritter Graham
May 12, 1897 – May 18, 1971

Isn't it reasonable to expect people at the mall to leave on their body parts?

I mean, *really* – is it TOO MUCH to ask that shoppers not remove limbs?

If you took a poll, everyone would agree that *no* one should *ever* take off a leg

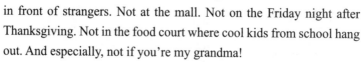

Chapter 1

in front of strangers. Not at the mall. Not on the Friday night after Thanksgiving. Not in the food court where cool kids from school hang out. And especially, not if you're my grandma!

No one shouted, "Off with her leg! Off with her leg!"

She volunteered!

She just took the thing off and started passing it around, as though it was a mall sponsored event, like Friday Night Show-and-Tell. She whipped off her favorite electronic hat – a seriously demented one with hula-dancing sunflowers – hiked up her quilted skirt, unbuckled her fake leg, and invited people to come over and take a look, up close and personal. She even showed off the purple amputation scar below her knee! I get the creeps just thinking about it, let alone make myself sick by marveling at how well the stitches have healed. But Grandma really, really, REALLY wants me to get used to it and accept her fake leg, as though it's some kind of pet, like our beagle puppy, Nose.

"Nose is our responsibility," she always says. "He's too expensive, won't stop howling, constantly escapes, steals everything edible, and is the only criminal we know, but at least he doesn't have fleas, is real cuddly, and most of all, Nose is *family*, so we have to accept him and love him just the way he is."

The same lecture fits Grandma's fake leg, except for the parts about howling, escaping, stealing, and being a criminal. If Grandma had her way, she'd include IT on our holiday cards: Best wishes, from Zinnia and Roland Weedervich (that's my mom and me), Sophie and Iris Zollo (that's Grandma and IT), and Nose. He's always last, but with his reputation, he's lucky to be included at all.

The thing that makes me mad is the way Grandma gets a loony

thrill out of ambushing me with all this. She knows I cringe whenever I see her scar, but she loves to take off Iris, her leg, and wave her stump at me at the weirdest times. I can't even walk through our kitchen without shielding my eyes in case she's painted a face on it, so it can tell me knock-knock jokes.

To be fair, the jokes aren't Grandma's fault. That's my mom's lunacy. As a professional puppeteer, she thinks a stump puppet might make physical challenges less scary to little kids. I don't see how, but Grandma's stump was a big hit at Mom's last preschool performance, so now she's writing a whole new show starring Grandma, her stump, and a leg named Iris. I can just imagine how it will be.

Little Red Riding Stump.

Stump and Iris meet Godzilla and King Kong: The Final Battle.

Riddles That Stump the Stump…

The next thing I know, they'll be asking me to build a portable closet for Iris' costumes. It's times like this that I hate being the man of the house. If Dad and Mom were still married, maybe Dad would put a lid on this creative madness, or at the very least, get stuck doing the carpentry.

The puppet show must have set off a dangerous chain reaction in Grandma's mind, because tonight was the first time she turned herself into a prosthetic exhibitionist. Suddenly *my* acceptance wasn't enough for her. Now she wanted unsuspecting shoppers to love Iris, too! And even though the mall is a twenty minute drive from Snowville, Ohio, my hometown, everyone gathered around Grandma just happened to go to my school.

They were the kids I've been avoiding all my life, the normal, dress-right, talk-right, think-alike crowd – the same loud mouth phonies who've been torturing me for years with *Reedy* Roland and *Wee Wee Weedy* jokes, which I might deserve a little, because let's face it, I can't expect *everyone* to ignore how I'm shaped exactly like string.

I'm your basic long and skinny kind of guy. Tall, pale, and thin. And my personality might be a little like string, too. Kind of twisted, plenty of knots, and frayed around the edges. My dad thinks I'm wound up too tight, too, but that's not exactly something I bring up in homeroom every day, if you know what I mean.

I hate to admit it, but this whole freak show with Iris only happened because I was ten minutes late. I was messing around with new demos and answering questions from other shoppers at the computer store. I thought it was no biggy that I stayed too long since I was hoping the manager would notice my skills and offer me a job as a junior consultant or something. I was supposed to meet Grandma in front of the Chinese place where they sell leftovers for half price at eight o'clock. You don't need a coupon or anything, but that didn't stop her from dragging along the portable file cabinet she calls her coupon saver. She claims she doesn't remember how she originally hurt her foot, but I think her coupon saver fell on it. Smashed it to smithereens.

Unfortunately, Grandma is not one of those sweet ladies who masks her deafness by speaking softly. She talks – or should I say, yells – loud enough for her to hear herself. So when I came running around the corner from the computer store, I heard her before I actually saw what she was up to.

"No, I'm not waiting for Reedy Weedervich," she shouted. "You have the first name wrong. I asked if you've seen *Roland* Weedervich."

Everyone was too dazed by Iris to see me duck behind a trash can.

"Yes, honey, Roland is my grandson. He and his mom have been living with me for about ten years, now. We were planning to eat Chinese food tonight, but it looks like they've already sold it all."

Geez! Put Iris back where she belongs!

"How? Did you say, how did I lose my leg? Well, they took it at the hospital. I went to get my diabetes checked and the next thing I knew, I woke up in the recovery room and my leg was gone!"

Not the body parts story!

"Someone must have needed a stubby little leg. But they'll be sorry they got mine with that awful black sore on my toe. I don't know how I got it, but it kept getting worse and worse, all gangrened. Roland kept telling me that I'd better get it checked. My doctor said that my toe rotted because of my sugar problem."

Please! Don't mention MY diabetes...

"What? What sugar problem? Is that what you said? Honey, you're going to have to speak up. You mumble just like my Roland. I can't hear him, either. Mumble, mumble, mumble, just like his mouth is always full. I keep telling him that he's going to end up just like me if he doesn't learn good eating habits while he's young. You can't tell by looking at him, he's so thin, but he has diabetes, too. Our bodies don't metabolize carbohydrate foods correctly, but Roland's mother is completely normal. She's my only daughter."

Oh, no! The stump puppet!

"You've never heard of Zinny's Zany Zoo, The Boom'n Bloom'n Puppet Brigade? Well, Roland's mother puts on lots of shows. His father is famous, too. He's that science fiction writer from New York, Latimer Weedervich? Roland's a sixth-grader at Snowville Middle School..."

Not my grades! Don't talk about my grades!

"How nice, you mean you all live in Snowville? My Roland has never gotten a grade lower than an A. Never even an A minus – now watch that you don't tear the stocking on my leg. Isn't it clever? Look, it's light brown, just like my eyes. Roland's eyes are light brown, too. And his mother's. All three of us have exactly the same coloring. Light brown eyes, light brown hair. Of course, my hair hasn't been brown for a few decades, but isn't it wonderful how they can make a leg look so real? I named it Iris after my favorite flower and did you know that Iris is a Rainbow Goddess, too? You should all come to see my gardens next spring. We live on..."

I *couldn't* let this go any further! But how could I stop her? *Think!* It was definitely time for Emergency Rule #1: Make the best use of what you have.

Panicking, all I could see was a blur of chairs, tables, and a bunch of bewitched bystanders. But then I remembered the trash can I was hiding behind. Before she could tell them where we live, I tipped it over and shoved it as hard as I could. It rumbled toward the group gathered around Grandma, picking up speed, getting faster and faster, like a boulder in an avalanche. Some girls turned around and screamed, "Watch out! Incoming trash!"

They scattered like pins in a bowling alley, but with them out of the way, the can hurtled straight at Grandma! I lunged forward and tried to kick it away, but I was too slow. It hit her bench, ricochetted off her coupon saver, knocked over her cane, blew its top, dumped its garbage, and finally skidded into a potted palm. It missed her real leg, and lucky for me, Iris was safely in the paws of a nosy stranger.

Grandma looked confused at all the commotion, but she smiled when her eyes finally focused on me. "Oh, Roland, I was just talking about you. You're late, you know. They've already sold all the Chinese food."

"Sorry," I mumbled. "I'll get salads instead."

My smirking tormentors snorted and exchanged sneers as they backed away, except for a tall pretty girl with a long, curly ponytail.

She couldn't leave.

She had Iris.

She hoisted Grandma's leg over her head like a victory trophy and gave her dark-brown bangs a feisty toss. "Cool grandma," she giggled. "Mine wouldn't be caught dead at the mall with me. She hates leaving Snowville for anything."

I must have been hypnotized by the silver braces that twinkled through her friendly smile, because all I could do was stand there and gaze into her shiny green eyes, completely paralyzed, like I'd been turned into a potted palm trimmed with unblinking, brown eyeball ornaments. I recognized her from school, but she was never in any of my classes and I was way too mortified to even try to think of her name. After all, I don't attack people with a loaded trash can every day.

Grandma leaned forward, straining to hear her voice, which was so soft and sweet, I could barely hear her, either. Her sleek wind jacket, blue and white like our school colors, swished as she stepped toward

Grandma. She was holding Iris with two hands, tennis racket style, as though she was getting ready to return a wicked serve across the food court. She glanced at me expectantly, her glowing face becoming more and more puzzled as the awkward silence grew longer and longer...

But I was struck mute, apparently zapped by some kind of deadly tongue-thickening disease. And then *everything* began to go wrong – tight throat – flipped stomach – face on fire. Oops! There went my knees. If I was online, I would have rattled off something smart and funny. But in person? The graffiti on the wall was more talkative than I could ever hope to be.

All I wanted was for Grandma to put Iris back on so I could pick up the stupid garbage and get the heck out of there. But then things got even worse! Out of nowhere, I heard a weeny little voice say, "Please pass Grandma's leg."

Oh, no! That weeny little voice was mine!

Instantly, my life flashed before eyes.

I was doomed.

No one – not in a million, zillion years – would *ever* forget a stupid comment like that.

At least, I wouldn't.

And now I have the rest of the Thanksgiving vacation weekend to think of a stop-them-dead-in-their-tracks comeback line before school on Monday.

It's a life or death situation.

The dilemma?

Think of a great comeback.

Or die.

I never thought I'd be glad about this because it's usually so annoying, but it's a good thing for me that Snowville is such a go-along-to-get-along kind of place. We Snowvillians want things to be normal so much that bold actions are practically illegal

Chapter 2

here. So there's a slim chance I might escape death by teasing, but only because it would be way too dramatic for this little town.

After all, what would people say?

The main attraction in Snowville is it's old-fashioned town square. Coffee sippers and ice cream lickers from all over Ohio like to hang out in the middle of town where a gazebo and gardens are surrounded by expensive boutiques that were grungy old thrift stores until a few years ago. That's when a rich land developer changed everything by publicizing Snowville as, "a trendy, up-and-coming suburb conveniently located a stone's throw from Cleveland, Ohio's second largest city…"

Before that, Snowville was just a farmer's market next to a bunch of historic houses. Then an army of architects showed up, waved a magic plan, said abraca-mansion, and *boom* – Snowville suddenly became "up-and-coming." But if you want to know the truth, *up and down* makes much more sense, since there's nothing but steep hills and rocky ravines all over town.

With trendiness, came new worries about what other people think. Survival now depends on saying exactly the right things to the right people at the right times while wearing exactly the right clothes in the right way – none of which I'm any good at. No one in my family is.

The only reason Snowvillians put up with us at all is that we got here first. Grandma's family arrived a hundred years before popularity became such a big deal. Now days, the old families are far outnumbered by the up-and-coming crowd. We live in small, decrepit houses and they live in expensive neighborhoods that were fields and woods when I started school just six years ago. My mom and I are amazed at how fast Snowville has changed, but Grandma is just plain dumbfounded. I wish that explained what happened at the mall tonight, but unfortunately, she was just being herself.

It's hopeless! She not only made me genetically incapable of fitting in, she had that same odd ball effect on my mom, too. Even Nose is on the weird side of quirky. Throw in diabetes, divorced parents, too many emergency rules, a tendency to be overly polite when I should be rude or moody, and – let's not forget – the great honor of being the skinniest sixth-grader in the whole state of Ohio – add them all up and you get a big, giant ABnormal! Worst of all, I hate being teased about all this stuff, especially since most of it's not my fault.

Grandma thinks it's okay to be thin-skinned as long as I say please and thank you and try real hard to love Iris. My mom says that I should stop worrying about what other people think and just try to be myself. Of course, she still wants me to worry about what *she* thinks. And my dad's solution to everything is to chill out and stop sweating the small stuff. But if actions speak louder than words, then Nose has the best advice of all. Just run away from everything.

Actually, until tonight, the first three months of sixth grade at Snowville Middle School haven't been that bad. I've been getting along better than ever, mainly because no one's been noticing me too much. Fifth grade at Erie Elementary was torture last spring when my diabetes was first diagnosed and I had to put up with tons of planning sessions and panicky visits to the nurse's office. Besides feeling crummy, the teachers treated me like I was a fragile freak and the cool kids thought I was weird *and* contagious. I couldn't wait to get out of there.

The middle school is bigger and more impersonal, so this fall, I've figured out how to quietly blend into the background of wherever I am, like I'm totally camouflaged. I guess you could say that I've been working on human invisibility and I've gotten pretty good at it, too. At least, I *was* pretty good at it until Grandma sabotaged me at the mall tonight. Now, thanks to her, I've not only been noticed, I've been discovered. And not in a good way, either.

Not in a good way at all.

The last time I came close to being discovered was five months ago in July when Nose was almost arrested for ravaging the Snowville U-Pick-M Raspberry Farm. Even though he's just barely a year old, he already has lots of bad habits, especially his

Chapter 3

obsessive urge to escape from wherever he is, just for the fun of it. He spends his whole day guarding doors, braced to pop out and run for his life as soon as they open. Unfortunately for me, the day he graduated from doors to van windows, was the day he began his life of crime.

My mom told me to open the window only an inch, but I said, "Don't worry. I'm holding Nose. He can't get away."

I know he did it just to spite me. As we were passing the U-Pick-M place, the little sleazeball wiggled loose, stretched his long neck out the window, thrust himself up and over, and looked as sleek as a chubby beagle could as he sailed away from our van. If Nose belonged to someone else, the sight of his front legs stretched forward and his back legs pulled straight back might have been awesome, like Super Beagle, to the rescue! But since he was mine, and I was the stupid idiot with the open window and empty lap, all I could do was yell, "NOOO!"

He landed square on his front paws and without even a stumble, began to howl a steady C-sharp as he charged into a tent that had been set up to shade the raspberries. He might have gotten off with a stern warning and a slap on the paw, but the tent was teeming with a bus load of white-haired ladies from Cleveland who couldn't tell a beagle howl from a fire alarm. They screamed and panicked, and then knocked over more tables than Nose. He got all the blame, though, because somehow those ladies knew they shouldn't frantically dart around gobbling up as many berries as their bellies could hold. And, unlike Nose, not one of them ran between anyone else's legs.

By the time we pulled in and parked, the tent was down, the ladies circled in a vengeful mob, and Nose was zinging through the raspberry plants with a dozen white-haired, red-fingered pickers chasing after him. He bobbed up and down, grinning and drooling, egging them on, and every couple seconds, he threw back his head to let out that high-pitched howl. The little show-off was having the time of his life bragging about winning his favorite game, Catch-Me-If-You-Can. The worst part was that Nose was just getting started and I knew he could go on like that forever, as long as someone was willing to play along.

I finally convinced everyone to stand still so I could bribe him with a treat, but the owner of the U-Pick-M Raspberry Farm, Alfred Trigger-Finger Rodriguez, had already called the Snowville police and reported Nose as a vicious animal. He was so mad, he rushed inside to get his rifle to put a stop to Nose's rampaging – permanently. But Mr. Rodriguez's temper was nothing compared to Grandma's. After we got home, she called him up and gave him a *few* pieces of her mind. Then she threatened to organize a raspberry boycott by rallying all the dog lovers in town, even the up-and-coming newcomers.

Old Trigger-Finger understood exactly who he was up against, since he and Grandma have been crosstown neighbors for practically a whole century. They went to high school together and some dances, too, since they were sweethearts before World War II lured him away and saved our family tree from becoming even more messed up than it already was. Anyway, it took a couple days for him to cool off, but he finally backed down and withdrew his complaint. Mom paid for all the smashed berries and replaced the ruined plants, and then I paid her. It all added up to ten mowed lawns and about fifty tons of dirty dishes, washed by you know who...

Nose's criminal vandalism was the only scandal that our monthly magazine, *The Snowville Drifter*, wrote about for the rest of the summer. Grandma was identified as Nose's owner, and since her last name is Zollo, (and mine is Weedervich) my invisibility wasn't damaged too much. But I had to answer tons of questions about how Nose could destroy so much so fast. There's no explaining this amazing skill of his, except to say that he's simply being himself, a beagle, one of the world's most energetic, hardheaded, and annoyingly playful breed of dogs, and one that naturally loves to hunt. The fact that he decided to go after raspberries that day was a little odd, but the police officers seemed to understand when they remembered who he belongs to.

I'm lucky this happened during July when school was out and most kids, especially the rich newcomers, were away on vacation. A week later, I left for upstate New York to stay with my dad, and I didn't get back until the end of August when it was finally time to board Moonman Fumesclinker's bus and enter the sixth grade.

A new start.

A new school.

Ruined!

How can being a measly ten minutes late cause so much trouble?

It's too bad I'm not as prompt as I am polite. Of course, if we had a law prohibiting all one-legged little old ladies wearing electronic hula-dancing hats from ever leaving their houses, then no one's life would be in total shambles right now...

Actually, there should be *lots* of laws!

And penalties, too.

I say, skip the trial!

Just lock them *all* up and throw away the keys!

Chapter 4

Every Saturday morning, I meet my dad online for a private chat. Our conversations are always the same. He asks what's going on, I say nothing. He tells me about the new chapters he's writing, I say that's good. He says he'll talk to me next week, I say bye.

But this Saturday, I'm desperate. I decide to clue him in on what happened last night on the outside chance he'll come up with a good idea for making it all go away. But as usual, he's not too impressed.

Dad: Don't you think you're exaggerating a bit?

Rol: Not this time. I have less than 48 hours to live.

Dad: Worse things have happened to me. Just last week I taught an entire class with my shirt tucked into my underwear – no belt – pink boxers hanging out the whole time.

Rol: No biggy. College students love underwear, the more, the better. Your pink shorts probably earned you a bonus.

Dad: No, only neon squirrels get bonuses. Pink is just – well, pink. Come to think of it, though, my boxers were white until I washed them with *your* red T-shirt last summer. Anyway, your grandmother's leg is her business. In America, we have the Constitutional right to remove and distribute our own body parts whenever we want. No laws were broken, right?

Rol: She told them about my diabetes, Dad. Do you know how sickening it is to be the only kid at school who has to have exactly timed meals and snacks, blood testing stuff, and all those stupid injections every single day?

Dad: No, but I do know something about being different. I like it.

Rol: But you get paid to be different. Having diabetes is the worst!

Dad: You got your diagnosis last March around your 11th birthday, didn't you? It's pretty rare for a guy your age, but you've been dealing with it just fine for almost 9 months. You'll be diabetic for the rest of your life. You know it's never going away.

Rol: Not until they find a cure. I'm hoping for a pancreas transplant or maybe an artificial one. For now, I want to keep it totally under wraps. But Grandma blabbed about it to everyone.

Dad: Don't you think everyone already knew?

Rol: No, especially not at my new school. I've been trying to go with the flow – you know, blend in. Be invisible.

Dad: All 60 inches of you?

Rol: All 63 inches. I gained weight and got taller with Dr. Greystone's diet.

Dad: You were only 5 feet tall when you left in August! Is it possible to grow 3 inches in 3 months?

Rol: I'm living proof. If I keep gaining 5 pounds for every inch I grow, I'll be a 6 foot tall, 160 pound lean mean machine by 9th grade.

Dad: If you keep working out.

Rol: So far so good. My morning blood sugar levels haven't skyrocketed for a long time.

Dad: Are you still injecting 3 times a day?

Rol: Yeah, but the more I exercise, the less insulin I have to take. Mom's on this diet, too, trying to make Grandma have better control.

Dad: Your grandmother's been doing the roller coaster thing her whole life. Her blood sugar up and down, hardly ever testing. My diabetic aunts were like that, too. One of them lost a leg, too.

Rol: I have nightmares that I'll end up like her. One-legged, half blind, huge robotic hats...

Dad: She's not all bad, son.

Rol: Yeah, only the parts you can see.

Dad: And talking about parts you can see, how can such a TALL guy like you be invisible?

Rol: Easy. No one sees me unless I say something.

Dad: Incredible. Silence creates invisibility? You want this?

Rol: Of course. You should see all the mansions sprouting up around here. We're being invaded by armies of spoiled rich kids.

Dad: Having money doesn't automatically make you bad.

Rol: Maybe, but I'm too late to get to know these new kids. Somehow everyone already got matched up.

Dad: And you don't have anyone?

Rol: Not in real face time.

Dad: You just need to join a few clubs at school.

Rol: Been there. Tried it. Didn't work.

Dad: Invite some kids over. Throw a party. Don't you always eat lunch with the same guys every day?

Rol: Yeah, the Brotherhood of Misfits – a junior scientist, a concert pianist, and a 300-pound Sumo. We could all play with Mom's puppets and then turn on Grandma's electronic hats to see which one wears down first...

Dad: How about going out for basketball? Isn't there a sixth grade team at school? You've got that lethal outside shot.

Rol: What if I get low blood sugar and pass out at practice?

Dad: Didn't Dr. Greystone teach you how to plan ahead for extra exercise?

Rol: Geez, Dad! Do we have to do this today?

Dad: OK, I'll get off your case, but you're not totally invisible. Your teachers notice you. Those advanced classes, your grades...

Rol: That's another thing! Grandma went on and on about that, too! I will NEVER survive this.

Dad: Roland, those kids at the mall don't care. It's not like they kept the leg or played Pig-in-the-Middle with it.

Rol: The trash can was like a garbage bomb.

Dad: But you didn't hit anyone...

Rol: PLEASE PASS GRANDMA'S LEG. That's what I said! No one will ever let me forget that STUPID comment!

Dad: Don't go ballistic on me. You're 11. Guys your age always overreact. Didn't only one person hear you say it?

Rol: Yeah, a girl.

Dad: Good looking?

Rol: Geez, Dad. Who cares? She could be Frankenstein and still look better than me. You'd better not tell Mom about this.

Dad: I won't, but what does she think about this whole leg thing?

Rol: The usual stuff about how well Grandma's adjusted to her tragic loss, on and on about what an important service she's providing to the community...

Dad: I get the idea. Your mother sees the sunny side of everything.

Rol: Yeah, and there's no use trying to explain why I'm so mad. She'd probably turn it into a puppet show.

Dad: And I'll use it in my next science fiction novel.

Rol: I'm trapped.

Dad: I hate to change the subject on you, but...

Rol: Wait! Help me think of something to say at school that will shut kids up when they tease me about what Grandma did.

Dad: You mean, about what YOU did? Pushing the can and that pass-the-leg comment? Those were your ideas, not her's. But if someone's dumb enough to mention it, how about saying something like, whatsit to yeah?

Rol: WHATSIT TO YEAH???? That's your best advice?

Dad: You could say, who cares.

Rol: WHO CARES????

Dad: It's true, isn't it? Truth is always best.

Rol: What about something wicked that will slay them before they slay me?

Dad: Just tell them to get a life.

Rol: That's not going to work.

Dad: OK, I'm sure you'll think of something. Anyway, I can't meet you in cyberspace next week.

Rol: What? You NEVER miss a Saturday.

Dad: I'm going to Iceland, remember? The English Department is sending me to the Third Annual Fairies, Elves, and Little People Conference in Reykjavik and my laptop is in the shop. Do you want me to telephone? I think Iceland is only a couple time zones further east of New York.

Rol: 5 time zones, Dad. It's close to the Prime Meridian. So if you call at noon from Iceland, it's 7 AM. in Snowville.

Dad: OK. I love you. Don't sweat this leg thing. It's not as bad as you think. All that matters is that the girl gave it back and that she's cute and single. You never know, your grandmother's leg might come in handy as irresistible chick bait one day…

Rol: For you, maybe. I'm not that sick. Have a good trip. I gotta go. I have a new E-mail coming in.

Dad: Wait! Start thinking about what you want to do during your school vacation next month. We'll have the last 10 days of December.

Rol: OK. Bye.

It's a typical lost-in-cyberspace Saturday morning. I exit Dad's private chatroom and open my new E-mail. It's a message from Warthog, my best cyberpal.

To: rw@dirtnet.utt.net
From: thehog@IOL.edu
Date: Nov. 27, 10:17 AM
Subject: mall gross out

Hey Dude. Can't meet 4 a private til next week. Got busted. Dad patrol, not cybercops. This granny leg thing sounds bogus. It's no biggy, U know? Who cares what a bunch of airheads think? Just tell em to get a life. I mean, whatsit to em? E me. The Hog

Now I've heard everything. The coolest guy in cyberspace has the same advice as my pink-shorted, college professor dad! My best defense on Monday morning are three of the weakest lines ever concocted by a guilty person.

Who cares?

Whatsit to yeah?

Get a life.

I'm dead.

I check my watch again. It's 7:32 AM, very cold, and still as dark as night. I'm standing two houses down and across the street from Grandma's, hiding behind the swirling cloud that covers my face every time I exhale. It's exactly what I need for

school today. A Fog Man mask. Now you see him, now you don't.

Whatever.

Nose is howling as loud as ever, begging to come along from inside our front door. Grandma says he carries on like that every day until my bus disappears around the corner. He's so good at throwing his voice, she's trying to get him booked on TV talk shows. Isn't that *just* what the world needs? Iris, Stump, and Nose: America's best-dressed leg, most-decorated scar, and loudest beagle ventriloquist. What a family.

When my bus finally pulls up, I'm relieved that my usual front seat is empty, but as soon as I step inside, I notice right away that it's weirdly quiet this morning. Either everyone is practicing my invisibility technique, or else they've all overdosed on too much turkey over the weekend. No one snores, beats out drum solos, or hums annoying little tunes. In fact, there's no evidence that anyone is even alive, except for maybe Moonman Fumesclinker, who works in school maintenance when he's not driving my bus. He doesn't say anything either, but with his jacket stretching up and his pants sagging down, I'm sorry to see that he's *more* than living up to his nickname today. Hurrah for extra large Fruit-of-the-Looms! And a short bus ride…

We unload in the parking lot and trudge gloomily up a ramp through the back door of Snowville Middle School, bunched together like slaughterhouse cattle. We have to pass the lunchroom in order to reach the main hallway, so there's no escaping the aroma of veggie paddies brewing in primordial ooze. Not a good sign.

Sixth-graders are assigned lockers in the main hallway near the Regurge-a-Dirge Factory, otherwise known as Principal Dirge's office. Mine is close to the bus loading ramp, so all I have to do is hang up my jacket, get my books, and join the single file line going up the narrow staircase leading to my homeroom on the second floor.

The tardy bell rings just as I plop down my book bag and slip into my seat. I'm hoping that Dad and Warthog are right about no one caring about Grandma's stupid leg, but just in case they're not, I avoid looking at anyone, and since I don't feel eyeballs drilling through the back of my head, I don't think anyone is looking at me, either. After a mumbled *Pledge of Allegiance*, we all collapse back down as Mr. Dirge clears his throat and begins his daily drone over the intercom.

"I trust that everyone here at Snowville Middle School had a safe and productive Thanksgiving weekend. Even though you may be distracted by the upcoming holidays, I want to make it perfectly clear that any interruptions to our regular schedule during the next three weeks will not be tolerated.

"Today's announcements. Item number one: all the boys' basketball teams finished their tryouts and the final rosters are posted *in* the gymnasium.

"Item number two: all girl basketball players will try out for one more day and should meet with Coach Gripp at precisely 3:37 PM *in* the gymnasium.

"Item number three: there are still two openings for Abominable Snowpeople. If you think you fit into the costume and would like to socialize with the winter cheerleaders, leave a completed application *in* the gymnasium. Remember, any middle school student, including sixth graders, may be considered.

"Believe it or not, item number four does not occur *in* the gymnasium…"

That's where he loses me. What a lousy way to start the day! As though things aren't already bad enough, now I have to be reminded first thing in the morning about how my stupid diabetes ruins everything! As one of the tallest sixth-graders, I should be on the Snowville Blizzards basketball team, but I'm nowhere close to knowing how to manage the extra blood sugar tests and insulin adjustments that would be required.

Figuring out gym class is challenging enough. If I work too hard, my blood sugar can get low, which is called hypoglycemia, a common side-effect of diabetes. If that happens, I have to eat something sweet right away, or risk passing out – something I'm desperate to avoid at school. But then again, if I don't exercise hard enough, or if we watch videos or have a written test, then my blood sugar can run too high. That makes me thirsty – nauseated – blurry-eyed – plus all the other horrible stuff high blood sugar causes.

Dr. Greystone thinks my diabetes will be more stable by spring when I can hopefully join the school track team. Meanwhile, Mom's been bugging me to apply to be an Abominable Snowperson. You have to wear a huge papier-mache head and shaggy monster suit during home games, but you take turns with the other mascots, so you only have to do it three or four times during the basketball season and once or twice at wrestling matches. I've been thinking that I might fill out an application today since no one would have to know it was me under that big...

Moonman's scratchy German accent crackles through the intercom and brings my mind back to homeroom. "Dis is Martin Fumesclinker. I got some news from dah maintenance department. All yooze kids gotta stay clear of dat boiler r-r-room in dah basement vile dat new trash-burning furnace is cranking. Yooze could get hurt messin' around down dare so yooze gotta stay out. And don't yooze forget! Help to save monies. Leave your garbage at school."

"I didn't know the old coot can speak English!" whispers a voice behind me.

"Yeah, but did you hear his voice crack? It fits the rest of him," snickers another.

"Yeah, *Moon*man..."

Even I had to smile at that one.

After some giggling and scuffling sounds, Emily Poplarski, the student council president, speaks next. "Um, hi everyone. Mr. Regur – I mean, Mr. Dirge called me at home during our day off from school last Wednesday? He said everyone broke their pencils in Mrs. Formula's algebra class at 1:19 PM last Tuesday? So we held an emergency meeting of the Student Conflict Resolution Committee at my house last Friday? We made this new, really sweet pencil policy? Sooo, starting today, no one in the whole building can use a pencil between one and two in the afternoon. Have a good one! Bye!"

Someone in the back cheers, "Yes! Perfect timing! No more fill-in-the-bubble with number-two-lead-pencil-only geography tests."

"No way," mutters someone else. "That new pencil thing won't last five minutes with Regurge-A-Dirge on the rampage."

Homeroom ends, so I shuffle off to my first class, study hall, and sign out for the library. So far, so good. I haven't had to say one word since I shouted good-bye to Grandma and Nose. I grab the new issue of *Teen Fitness* and sneak into the back storeroom where decades of accumulated library junk covers a wooden table and overflows onto a bunch of broken down chairs. I push aside a stack of tattered magazines and move a moldy box. Flesh-eating bacteria and nitpicking cooties thrive in here, so just to be safe, I wipe off the table with my sweatshirt sleeve before sitting down, propping up my feet, and opening to the classified ad section in the back of the magazine. Maybe some enterprising genius invented an artificial pancreas...

"Reedy? Or is it Roland? You're only a sixth-grader, aren't you? And in all those brainy accelerated classes? I thought..."

Ah oh. Red alert! Enemy intruder! Arm the torpedoes! Prepare to launch the killer comeback line!

Get ready.

Aim.

Darn it! What was that stop-them-dead-in-their-tracks thing I was going to say? *Think!* Oh, yeah...

The voice keeps talking, "...I thought your name was *Reed*, but then Friday night your grandma mentioned Roland, so I'm sorry, but I'm not sure what to call you..."

"Whatsit to yeah?" I grumble, looking back toward the library for the first time.

Oops! Misfire! It's the cute girl with the curly ponytail! I should have recognized that soft voice of her's. And she's giving me that look again. Glowing face – pretty eyes – friendly smile.

Does she want something?

Or someone?

Is it me?

Chapter 6

"What do you mean, whatsit to yeah?" she says with a toss of her bangs.

"Oh – um – I don't know. I mean, who cares what you call me?" I notice CRYSTAL NELLSON drawn in big, loopy rainbow colors on the back of her notebook.

"It matters to me. I hate being called Cristy, or even worse, Crystaline. That's my real name, can you believe it? Crystaline?"

"That's not so bad, not like *my* middle name."

"It can't be worse than Crystaline."

"Oh, it is. Believe me, it's *much* worse."

"Impossible."

"All right, you tell me. Isn't Wilbur as bad as it gets?"

She grins. "You weren't named for that pig in *Charlotte's Web*, were you?"

"One of my mom's favorite characters."

She laughs and steps closer to my table. "Okay, you win. Wilbur beats Crystaline, but it gets pretty boring listening to fifty million verses of 'Oh my darlin, Oh my darlin, Oh my darlin, Crystaline' all the time."

She rolls her eyes and huffs with disgust. "You wouldn't believe how bad most people sing."

I can't help noticing that her singing isn't too great, either, but amazingly, I don't mind. "So, you're Crystal?"

She nods. "And you're Roland?"

I shrug. "I guess. It's no biggy."

"No one ever comes back here in the morning, do they?"

I shake my head.

"So we can talk without anyone hearing?"

I nod.

"It's not that I mind being seen with a sixth-grader, 'coz I know lots of younger kids. Older ones, too. It's just that I don't know how I'm going to survive at school today!"

And then without any warning, she drops her notebook onto the table, kneels in the wobbly chair across from me, presses her face into her arms, and collapses just as I yank my size tens out from under her.

This is, without a doubt, the most stunning thing I've ever seen at school. Not close to something Grandma would pull, but right up there with one of the most unexpected surprises of all time. Why would an overwrought Clementine-singing *older* babe plop herself down in the middle of my hideout and have the world's quietest nervous breakdown? She was perfectly normal two seconds ago.

I look down and try to read my magazine, but who can concentrate with a flipped-out silent person in front of you? She obviously needs some time to recover, so I count to ten. Slowly. But she still doesn't move. Finally, I lean toward the human heap sprawled on the table, clear my throat, and say, "Um, hello in there… Are you okay?"

She sniffs softly, her narrow shoulders shuddering. Then a tear rolls out onto the table. It's a big one – maybe a world's record. Practically a lake. Splash! There's another. Two lakes…

Great. Silent crying. What am I supposed to do now?

"Um, Crystal? Is someone picking on you?"

She looks so pathetic that I'm starting to get furious at whoever's hurting her, but I'm kind of relieved, too. She's definitely got more going on than my trash can escapade. After what seems like the longest wait of my life, she finally untangles her right hand, pulls a tissue out of her front jean pocket, and blows her nose so hard, her rickety chair starts to rattle.

I swallow and take another stab at it. "Geez, I thought I had problems. I mean, *your* grandma didn't pass her leg around at the mall, too, did she?"

She snorts a surprised laugh, but then covers her mouth and starts to cry again. This time, high-pitched squeals escape as wisps of wavy dark hair fly up around her ears.

Okay. *Think!* Isn't there an emergency rule for consoling babes in distress? I consider warning her about the flesh-eating bacteria and nitpicking cooties next to her face, but thankfully, her sobbing spell ends before I have to say anything. She inhales shakily and looks up at me, but I avoid her miserable eyes by staring instead at the crooked red line that's been pressed across her nose.

"This is a big mistake," she sighs, unfolding one leg and pushing herself half out of her chair. "I don't even know you. And you're just a sixth-grader. It's dumb to bother you with my problems."

"No, that's okay. Bother me. I mean, it's not dumb."

Her watery eyes burn through mine while she decides whether to stay or run. It's like a staring contest, my dry brown against her wet green, and I'm dying to blink. She finally loses by looking away, and then she sniffs, eases herself back down, and leans toward me.

"I was planning to skip all my classes today," she croaks. "I was looking for a place to hide, but when I saw you sitting here, I remembered what your grandma said about your grades and I thought that maybe someone smart like you might be exactly who I need right now. I've done a terrible thing and I don't know how to make it better."

"It can't be that bad."

"It's worse than anything you could ever imagine."

"Don't tell me. You broke your braces, right? Or did your dog eat a library book? Oh, I know, you got caught talking about a friend and now she's never going to speak…"

"My mom was arrested because of something I did."

Her face scrunches into a silent scream as she presses her hands over her ears and shakes her head violently, her chair rocking dangerously with each toss of her long ponytail.

"Stop it! If someone looks in, they'll think you're going to explode!" Without even thinking, I reach across the table and grab her wrists.

She sucks in a deep breath and freezes like a statue. "It's all my fault," she says without moving her lips. "The Snowville police came and got her yesterday."

"Is she still in jail?"

She shakes her head, yanks her wrists back, and reaches for another tissue. "They let her come home last night. But then the superintendent of schools called and told her not to come to work today. She'll probably be fired and go to prison, all because of me!"

I glance at her notebook again. Crystal *Nellson*. "Does your mom work in our lunchroom?"

She nods. "She's the manager. She said that it's all a big mistake, but she doesn't know how bad things are."

My imagination goes wild. "Are we infested with rats? E-coli bacteria? Poisoned mustard? I always knew it smelled…"

She rolls her eyes and interrupts, "I wish it was something simple like that."

"What could be worse?"

"Stealing." Crystal nearly chokes on the word.

"Mrs. Nellson? I mean, your mom? A thief? No way. She's one of the only truly decent people at school. She's on my school health team and always makes sure that my lunch fits this new diet I'm on."

"They have evidence. They found school food at our house."

"How did it get there?"

"That's the worst part! I put it there!"

"You stole food from our school?"

"Noooo," she wails. "And neither did my mom!"

"I don't get it, Crystal. You put stolen food in your house, but you didn't steal it and neither did your mom. So who did?"

"That's exactly why I need your help! Who did? Who stole the food and how can we convince the Snowville police that my mom is completely innocent and should have her job back right away!"

"It sounds easy, Crystal. Just tell them where you got it. What did they find at your house, anyway?"

"Mock chicken legs."

"You mean those little speckled orange things that look like flat light bulbs?"

"Exactly. There were big potato flakes, too."

"That grainy white stuff?"

"Yep. In a ten pound bag."

"Whoa. Anything else?"

"Tuna. A big box full of giant cans."

"That's it? Sacked potatoes, yucky light bulb things, and a bunch of Gargantuan tuna? Where did you get them?"

She takes a deep breath and stares at the shelves behind me, shaking her head, mystified. "It was so *weird*. Last Wednesday, you know the day before Thanksgiving when we were off from school? I was shooting hoops in our driveway when a white pickup truck pulled up. A guy asked if this was where Opal Nellson lived. He said that he had some food for her and that she'd know what to do with it. He had this huge box of mock chicken legs and he said I should put it in the freezer right away. I said okay and then he offered to help."

"You let him into your house?"

"No, our freezer is in the garage, and the door was already open, so he just followed me. I lifted the lid and he put it in. He covered it with packages of frozen raspberries. Then he got another box out of his truck, and said that I should put it somewhere safe. I asked him if under the kitchen sink was okay and he said fine, as long as it didn't get wet. When I came back outside, he was gone."

"Did your mom know what to do with it like he said?"

"Who knows? I forgot to tell her. I'm trying out for the Lady Blizzards basketball team, so that's where my mind was. I practiced during the whole vacation, except Friday night at the mall when I saw you. We had loads of relatives over on Thanksgiving and then my dad had extra work for all of us. We own Mel's Stables…"

"Next to the Snowville U-Pick-M Raspberry Farm?"

"Yep, that's my grandpa's farm."

"Your grandpa is Trig – I mean, Alfred Rodriguez?"

She nods. "Do you know him?"

"Not as well as *some* members of my family."

"He's my mom's dad. When my parents moved back to Snowville, he gave them ten acres from his farm so my dad could start a horse boarding business. That was way before I was born, but it was about the same time that my mom started working for the schools. Anyway, Dad's business is having a real hard year. A competing stables opened by Kings Forest."

"You mean that new neighborhood next to the highway?"

"Yep, and this weekend, lots of our renters moved their horses over there. My mom and dad were real busy with all that, and worried, too, with tuition payments for both my sisters due pretty soon. Then yesterday while we were fixing turkey sandwiches, the police showed up with a search warrant. They went right to the freezer and under the sink, exactly like they *knew* where to look. I tried to explain but they told me to stay home and be quiet."

While I'm listening to every detail, I'm also trying to block out guilty thoughts about her grandpa, Trigger-Finger Rodriguez. I decide that she must not know that Nose, the infamous raspberry hound, is mine, and I'm wondering if I should tell her before she confides anymore. But instead, I point out the obvious.

"This is a no-brainer, Crystal. Just ask the delivery guy to tell them what happened."

"There's more. The police have computer records that show lots of missing food. They said it might be worth over $10,000!"

"$10,000 for disgusting light bulb things, fake spuds, and giant tuna?"

"And other stuff. Lots and lots of other stuff."

"You've got to find that delivery guy. Did you get his name?"

She shook her head.

"What did he look like?"

"He wore a brown uniform and was real thin and pale like he was sick, or something. He was even skinnier than you. The main thing I remember were his teeth."

"What? Vampire fangs?"

"Yeah, right, and he bit me and now I'm his eternal slave... Come on, Roland, I'm not kidding around."

"Okay, already. So what's with his teeth?"

"Some were missing, from both the top and the bottom. I noticed 'coz my grandpa's missing some teeth, too."

"That should make him easy to spot."

"If the police believe me."

Just as I'm about to ask her what she wants *me* to do, the bell rings and the librarian ducks in to tell us to hurry back to class.

"Call me tonight after basketball tryouts," she pleads.

"Me call you? Um, I can't… well… um, maybe… I mean, yeah, I guess. Are you going back to class?"

She nods and rubs her face while she slips away into the crowded hallway.

No one else notices me for the rest of the morning. I identify the capital of Peru in geography class and say, 'Here's my abominable application' to the lady in the athletic office, but other than that, zip. Either Dad and Warthog are right about no one caring about Grandma's leg, or else my invisibility shield is working perfectly. I don't even need the Fog Man mask.

Something definitely has to be done to help Mrs. Nellson, though. She never makes a fuss about my special lunch, but some other lady is in charge today and she set my tray off to the side labeled with a huge sign that's slightly bigger than the Statue of Liberty.

> ROLAND WEEDERVICH
> ***DIABETIC***

Flashing neon lights wouldn't make it more noticeable!

I consider skipping lunch so I won't have to figure out where to hide it, but that would mess up my blood sugar for the rest of the day. So I grab my tray and stash the stupid sign under my sweatshirt as I slink over to the B.O.M. section, a small square table in the back that's closest to the Regurge-a-Dirge Factory. It's where the Brotherhood of Misfits hangs out at lunch. If some rotten jerk turns us into a target, at least there's a chance he'll be spotted from the office. Not that getting caught really matters, though.

At Snowville Middle School, we're expected to handle our own *social problems.* But none of us in the B.O.M. can figure out where a social problem ends and a bullying problem begins. The "just kidding" remark seems to work as a universal excuse for doing whatever you want, so it's pointless to even try to get any adult help. Plus, you don't get into the B.O.M. section unless you stink at making small talk, so we don't exactly spend our lunch periods energetically mapping out anti-jerk strategies. I hate to admit it, but we're such hopeless losers, we don't even speak up to help each other.

I nod a greeting to the same three guys who are always here, Jerome Bell, imperial wizard of science fairs, Sam Lu, piano prodigy, and Kevin Heel, the fattest kid you've ever seen. If you look at him with your right eye and me with your left, your brain perceives us as one average-sized kid. But we're not discussing optical illusions, today. As usual, we're not discussing anything. Like monks committed to silence, we all simply study our food and shovel it in, relieved to have these few peaceful moments at school where each of us finally *belongs.*

Chapter 7

I've never called a girl before. Not about a homework assignment, not about diabetes, not about finding a runaway Nose, not about anything… So naturally, Crystal's parting words put me under some kind of spell. Calling her is all I can think about for the rest of the day and by the time I board Moonman's bus for my ride home, it's starting to really bug me that she was so casual about asking me to do it. For all I know, she left me and poured her heart out to fifty other guys, all of them popular, with two-legged grandmothers and well-mannered dogs.

I don't even know when tryouts end. Should I call Coach Gripp and ask when Superstar Crystal Nellson will be free to take a very important phone call? And then if I figure out when to call, I'll probably get busy signals for hours. All those fifty guys clogging up the lines. And anyway, what do you say to an older girl on the phone? Especially one that's practically a stranger.

Good evening, madame. This is Roland W. Weedervich. May I please speak to Miss Crystaline?

No, too polite, even for me.

Hi. Is Crystal there?

No, too relaxed for this stolen food business.

Hello. Is Crystal home from basketball yet?

No, too familiar. Whoever answers might say, 'Whatsit to yeah?' I'd probably blurt out something stupid like, 'Just tell her to get her butt to the phone!' and then get myself slammed for life.

What if she's not home when I call? Should I leave a message? If I leave my name, will Mrs. Nellson realize that I let Nose destroy her father's raspberries? What if Mr. Nellson answers and gets mad because he doesn't want Crystal talking to boys?

No, Crystal wouldn't do that to me.

Or would she?

An even worse problem is how to make the call without Mom

finding out, because when it comes to parents, keeping them ignorant is the *only* way to go. With Dad living 400 miles away, he's no trouble at all. He's more like a cyberpal than a parent. But Mom's trickier. Snap judgements rule her world. She snoops out facts and draws conclusions before normal people even suspect something's going on. And when she gets worried, watch out! Like the close call I had last spring – she opened Warthog's E-Mail and got *real* suspicious *real* fast. We were into abbreviations back then and our messages looked like coded gobbledygook. Without any warning, she called the FBI *and* threatened to cancel our online account, right then and there.

It's a good thing I was close by. I leaped into action and followed Emergency Rule #2: Always make parents think you're on their side. I slapped on my most cooperative smile and deciphered his message as fast as I could. It turned out to be a no-vowel riddle.

Mom's heart stopped climbing up her throat as soon as I figured out that a black cat had crossed under the St. Louis Arch. She was so relieved, she practically

| ST L (^) |
| BLK CT X |

gave me a medal for helping poor Warthog with his communication problems. Now she doesn't bother with him at all, which is lucky for me, since no one in cyberspace knows more about keeping parents ignorant than The Hog.

I met him over a year ago in a computer tech chatroom. Most chatters want your vitals before wasting any words on you, but he's never asked for anything. Neither have I. And anyone who uses Warthog as a screen name can't be too cute, so we probably have ugliness in common, along with lots and lots of other stuff. It's risky to operate without visuals, though. He could be anyone in real life, even a perverted ax-wielding one-legged grandma. I seriously doubt it, though, because perverts always beg for pictures. Plus, I don't think he has a real life.

He says he's fourteen, lives near St. Louis, Missouri, and is thinking about dropping out of high school to stop his dad from yanking his computer time whenever his grades aren't perfect. Mostly he keeps his dad in the dark, but if he ever slips up, it's no biggy since he's also great at making teachers accept extra credit they don't really want. He's funny, but he's kind of a cyberholic nut case, too. I mean, I'm socially invisible, too skinny to have a shadow, and live with the planet's most bizarre people, but at least I have a little bit of a life away from my machine.

There's Nose to chase after. And diabetes to manage. And there's always that phone call this afternoon…

Maybe I *should* tell Mom about Crystal. It might give her something to worry about besides my blood sugar or how much time I spend online. One minute she brags about my skills, but the next, nags about my obsession. And whenever she hears about crime on the Internet, she invents long, lame lists.

MUST Do Before Computer is Used Again

Clip coupons	Enroll Nose in obedience school
Sort coupons	Replace batteries in Grandma's hats
File coupons	Polish Iris

Top Priority Family FUN!!!

Join Diabetes Support Group	Go garage sailing
Make egg carton puppets	****Visit zoo****

I haven't *enjoyed* going to the zoo since I was five. The last time Mom mentioned that it was a nice day to visit orangutans, I talked her into surfing the Net with me instead.

Starting with the Star Battle web site was the smartest thing I'd done in ages. It has zillions of animated graphics and high-tech videos that take *forever* to load through our old modem. Mom loves the Star Battle puppets, but she's the touchy-feely type. If she can't squeeze something, smell it, turn it upside down, inside out, and eventually throw it in the washing machine, she's not very interested. She tried every link, but after a fidgety hour, she weaseled away by diabolically faking a bathroom attack.

It wasn't a total bust, though. After waiting for all those graphics to download, she offered to buy me a faster modem, which I really, really wanted, but was afraid to ask for, since we're not exactly rolling in piles of extra cash. Basically, we get by with Grandma's pension and whatever Mom earns in her puppet business. Sometimes they both work weekends passing out samples in grocery stores and Dad sends a monthly check for me, but with two diabetics and so many battery-gobbling hats in the family, we have lots of extra expenses.

I figure that as long as we can afford unlimited, unrestricted Internet access, I can put up with almost anything. So I never buy stuff online and let Mom join me only when I have to, like when she looks like she's about to make a new list, which is exactly what she'll do if she finds out about me calling Crystal. It'd be just like her to slip me the top ten things teenage girls like to talk about before I even have time to punch in Crystal's phone number.

And then she'd make another list about proper phone etiquette.

And another on the do's and don'ts of teenage dating…

That would be torture. No, it'd be *worse* than torture. So with a list-making mother like mine, I have no choice. I *have* to sneak around and make this a stealth phone call, totally beyond her radar.

As soon as I get home, I'll do all my usual after school stuff, like raid the fridge, check my E-mail, play with Nose, and crank up the radio in my room until Crystal has enough time to get home from tryouts. When Mom and Grandma are busy in the kitchen, I'll mosey into the living room to use the phone that's attached to our computer system. I'll call Crystal. Once. If she doesn't answer, or if the line is busy, I'll hang up and forget about it. I won't leave a message and I won't try again.

It's a perfect plan.

But when I step off Moonman's bus and head up Western Reserve Avenue toward home, the booming uproar blasting out of Grandma's house warns me that things won't be working out quite so well.

Plan B? Where are you? I need you!

Now!

Chapter 8

"Thief! Thief!"

Crash

"I'll get you!"

WoooooooWooooo

"You can't get away from me!"

Walking into our foyer is like stepping into rush hour traffic. I'm nearly flattened as Grandma zooms by in my computer chair, the wheels attached to the bottom screeching like someone's sick cat.

"Roland! Shut the door! Don't let the beast escape!"

The chair stops, so Grandma spreads her arms like eagle wings and slaps her open palms against the walls. *Whack*, and she's off again, rolling and squealing down the hallway toward the kitchen.

"Grandma! Is there a burglar here?"

She drags her heel across the floor in order to slow down and turn into the kitchen. "Where are you, you dirty little rat?"

That's when I hear something like a stampede coming from the living room to my left. Oh, no! It's beagle mania! Nose is a flash of black, white, and tan as he leaps onto the couch, sprints along its full length, and then whips around to race the other way. He flings himself off, tumbles onto the carpeted floor, scampers under the coffee table, vanishes behind the couch, pops out on the other side, and then, like a rocket, launches himself straight toward me.

"Settle down, boy!"

I slam the front door and throw down my book bag just as his paws strike the linoleum in the foyer, making him skid head first into my knees. He grunts, rolls over, then trumpets out a long C-sharp.

"Nose! Stay!"

He jumps up and clamps onto my thigh, wildly wagging his tail and franticly licking my hand. I try to grab his collar, but he twists away and pushes off, knocking me backwards into the doorknob.

Grandma uses the kitchen table to spin herself around, then pushes off and glides back into the hallway, trapping Nose between us. He tries to charge at her, but he's too frenzied to get his footing on the polished floor. Finally he digs in and springs onto her lap, licks her mouth, and then climbs over her shoulder onto the kitchen counter.

"Aaarrrgh! Get down from there!" she screams, wiping her lips with her sleeve.

He sniffs everything on the counter before dismounting. Then he squeezes under Grandma's chair, flops down in the hallway between us, and belts out a self-satisfied howl.

Beagle joy + Grandma rage = PURE CHAOS.

It's the perfect formula for ruining the perfect plan.

I glance at Grandma. She's trembling and breathing hard, her face deadly pale. I've never seen her this angry before.

"Chasing him always makes him wilder, Grandma," I mumble as I turn back toward the door to get my book bag.

"I know, but he stole Iris! I had those phantom pains again, so I took a pain pill and laid down on the couch to watch my stories on TV. I fell asleep and when I woke up, Iris was gone!"

"How long have you been trying to catch him?"

She shakes her fist at Nose. "Too long, honey. Much too long."

"Where's Mom?"

"She went to get her new promotional brochures from a printer in downtown Cleveland."

"Don't look so proud of yourself," I say to Nose as I step past him and spin Grandma around toward the kitchen. I'm surprised to see her insulin supplies scattered all over the counter. She never leaves them out like that. I start to get a bad feeling that there's more wrong with her than just a lost leg.

"How did you get over to my computer chair?" I ask her gently.

"I crawled across the living room floor. It wasn't hard."

"So you didn't have your walker?"

"Of course not! Why would I? I was wearing Iris." Her eyes are still smoldering and if I'm not careful, I'll catch it next.

"Should I push you over to the kitchen table?"

She exhales an irritated huff. "I suppose, but first, I want you to strangle that little dog."

"Then we'll never find your leg."

I steer her chair to the table and sit down, too. Her glassy brown eyes stare past me as her damp face starts to wobble, as though her head is attached to a fragile spring. She looks like a life-sized bobble-head Grandma doll. Not exactly a collector's item…

"What have I done to deserve these troubles?" she asks in a strained, raspy voice. "I cooked and cleaned for your grandpa for forty-two years, bless his heart, so quiet and humble, no one ever guessed what a wonderful man he really was. So shy, so painfully shy…"

"Grandma? Are you sick?" I ask, sneaking a peek back toward the uncapped syringe and loose cotton balls on the counter.

She groans, trembling. "You don't understand."

I try my hardest to sound calm and diplomatic. "I'm only asking because you don't usually sleep during the day."

"I already *told* you. My foot was aching like it was *still there*."

"Your voice – you don't sound like yourself."

Sparks fly from her eyes again. "And who do you think I am? The big bad wolf? Are you Little Red Riding Roland?"

"Don't get mad. How about if I heat some water for tea?"

Instead of answering, her shoulders sag as she turns to stare out the window into the back yard. "Your grandpa was tall and lean like you, Roland. You're getting more like him all the time."

Feeling panicky, I fill a kettle and put it on the stove, turning the dial to high, trying to remember the last time she acted like this. Sad, mad, confused, all at once. I'm afraid she's having an insulin reaction. Hypoglycemia. Too much insulin, too little blood sugar. I've been like this, too, but it's different watching someone else have symptoms. One thing's for sure, though. If I don't help her right away, she could have a convulsion or go into shock. Maybe even die. But what if I'm wrong? What if she's just in a wacky mood?

Think. What am I supposed to notice when I'm feeling edgy?

When my diabetes was diagnosed last March, Dr. Greystone made me memorize the symptoms of low blood sugar and then he drummed on his desk and made demented percussion sounds while I sang this rap song, over and over, into an old stethoscope.

Drowsy. Pale. Shaky. Confused.
Sweating. Hungry. Heart overused.
Numb tips. Dizzy. Lips-a-tingle.
Hy-po-gly-ceeeeem-eee-ah. Yeah!

Grandma's definitely tired, trembling, pale, and sweating. But how can I tell if she's got tingling lips or a racing heart? She's acting weird, but if I'd been trying to catch Nose by wheeling around in a screechy computer chair all day, I'd be bonkers by now, too. Wouldn't anyone?

"Grandma? Are you hungry?"

"*What*, Roland? Speak up."

"Do you want something to eat?" I shout.

"Do I want some *feet*? What kind? Pickled or fried?"

This is not going well. "When is Mom coming home?" This time, I'm loud enough for the neighbors to hear.

"Some time next week."

"Did you mean today or next *week*?"

She doesn't answer, so I grab a slice of turkey from the fridge and go to sit across the table from her. "I see your insulin stuff is still out on the counter. Did you inject your second dose after lunch?"

She knits her eyebrows. "Yes, I think so…"

"Are you dizzy? What did you eat today?"

And then without any warning, she flies off the handle and slaps the table with both hands. "You little know-it-all!" she hollers, her eyes blinking rapidly. "You're just like your mother, always checking on me, looking for candy wrappers, grabbing food out of my hands. I've lived with diabetes for thirty-five years. You have it since March and you think you're an expert! How dare you?"

With typical bad timing, Nose trots into the kitchen and zeros in on my turkey, totally mesmerized. If dogs had telekinesis, it'd be in his mouth by now. I scowl and stomp my foot, so he slinks away to beg from behind the family room couch.

I wait a few seconds, and then try again. "Grandma? Please, I'm just trying to help. I think you're low."

"Leave me alone. I'm too tired to think about it right now." She mops her face with her sleeve and gazes out the window again.

"If you forgot to eat, or if it wasn't enough…"

"*I don't know.* I took a pain pill. My soap opera was coming on."

"Your story comes on at 1:30, right?"

"No, it was a couple days ago."

"*Days*? That doesn't make sense. Did you take your insulin before or after your pain pill?"

"Either one, or both would be fine. Help me to my room, dear."

"Okay, Grandma. I'll get your walker."

But instead, I hurry into the bathroom next to the kitchen to get my blood testing kit. I have a spring-loaded finger pricker that I use several times a day. It lets me get a blood sample without poking too deep or hurting too much. I have to squeeze a drop onto a test strip and put it into an electronic meter that measures how much sugar is in my blood. If there isn't enough blood sugar, I have to eat something sweet right away. If there's too much, I have to inject insulin. I carry identical monitoring and injecting supplies with me in my book bag at school and Grandma has the same stuff, only she doesn't test as often as she should. It's why she lost her leg. I *can't* let anything else happen to her.

"Hurry, Roland. I think I'm going to faint."

I tear open a new lancet for my finger pricker, but my hands are shaking worse than Grandma's, so I drop it and have to get another. I finally get a good grip, insert it, peel off a new test strip, and then bring it all out to the kitchen table.

"Grandma, I'm going to test your blood sugar." I take her index finger, pop the lancet, and squeeze a drop of blood onto the test strip before she can pull away.

"I'll be right back."

I take the test strip back to the bathroom where her old meter is plugged into an outlet by the sink. In just a few seconds, it beeps and flashes a dangerously low reading! I have to make her drink something sweet right away, like regular pop or orange juice. Then I'll test her again to see if her reading's back to normal.

I leave the test supplies in the bathroom, get a pitcher of orange juice from the fridge, pour some into a small glass, and stir in an extra spoonful of sugar. Steam is shooting out of the whistling teapot, so I shut off the stove before going back to Grandma.

"Roland, what's taking so long?"

"Here I am. Your sugar is real low. Drink this and then you probably won't even feel tired anymore."

"All right, honey. Then will you look for Iris?"

"I'll check all of Nose's hiding places."

She drinks the juice and then smiles at me, calmer already. "Do you think chasing Nose is too much exercise for a one-legged old lady like me?"

"Chasing Nose is too much exercise for anyone. You shouldn't have gone after him like that."

"I almost caught him, but he's a slippery little thing."

"How long has my computer chair doubled as a race car?"

She chuckles. "Do you remember when your mother measured our doors and hallways and found out that they were too narrow for the wheelchair the therapists recommended? We couldn't afford the renovations, so she thought this chair might work just as well."

"We're lucky she wasn't thinking about puppets that day or my chair would be a fire-breathing dragon by now. You're not shaking anymore. How's your heart rate?"

"Fine, honey. I feel better already."

"You should measure your blood sugar again."

"Yes, I'll do it after a while."

"Do you want some tea? The water's hot."

"Not yet."

"Did I do the right thing? I mean, about the testing and the juice?"

"Yes, Roland, you did fine, just like always." She reaches for my hand and strokes it gently. "Thank you, honey. I'm sorry I was so ornery."

"I was pretty scared. It's weird how someone else being low is worse than when you're low yourself. That must be how Mom feels all the time. She sees us acting differently, but doesn't exactly know why."

She nods and squeezes my hand. "Have I ever told you about how your diabetes is all my fault?"

I pull my hand away and glance out the window, glad that a bunch of blue jays and cardinals are battling for the best spot at the bird feeder. At least I'll have something entertaining to look at while Grandma goes on and on about my all-time least favorite subject.

"If my mother didn't have diabetes, then I wouldn't have it, and you, Roland, wouldn't have it, either," she says, mechanically reciting the same words I've heard dozens of times during the last nine months.

"Sometimes I worry that I shouldn't have had children at all," she continues. "When my first baby was born dead, maybe that was a sign that I shouldn't become a mother at all."

"But you didn't have diabetes then, did you?"

"No, not until after your mother was born."

"So you didn't know."

"I should have warned your mother more, though. She grew up watching my diabetes get worse and worse. She should have known better than to marry someone who has so much diabetes in his family, too. I'll never forget the morning she called to tell me she married that father of yours. He was just a long-haired, unemployed New York hippy in those days. And Weedervich? No offense to you, Roland, but what kind of name is that? They didn't even have a real wedding. Just a simple visit to city hall. No reception. He said he didn't believe in all that nonsense."

"I've heard this story a million times, Grandma. Dad and Mom both say that getting married was the happiest and dumbest thing they've ever done."

She laughs. "Well, it's usually not very smart to run out and marry someone you don't get along with, even if you *think* you're in love. But if they weren't so impulsive, we wouldn't have you, would we, Roland?"

I swallow hard and look away. Even though they've been divorced for as long as I can remember, it still hurts to think how much easier my life would be if my parents shared at least a couple interests. As it is, I'm the only thing they have in common.

"At least they're still nice to each other," I say, feeling defensive. "Some kids have to put up with all kinds of fighting."

"Yes, but you have the bad luck to have diabetes on *both* sides of the family," she adds as she reaches over to rub my back.

"But that doesn't matter," I say, squirming away. "Dr. Greystone says that mine's probably not inherited. No one knows for sure what causes Juvenile Diabetes. They think it might start from a virus that makes my own body attack itself, not anything related to you or Dad or his aunts or your mother…"

"Yes, honey, that's true. Type I diabetes like yours doesn't always have a family connection. Not like mine." She sighs and shakes her head sadly. "Your grandpa was in and out of the hospital with terrible cancer treatments just after you were born, and the worse he got, the worse I managed my blood sugar. When you were just a toddler and you and your mother came to help after he died, I never expected that you'd stay. But I'm sure glad you did."

She pauses, her brown eyes moist and tender. "You don't like me talking about all this, do you Roland?"

I shrug.

"Well then, I simply can't say another word until my leg is found…"

"I'd better get busy then!"

I jump up and whistle for Nose to follow me into the living room. He sniffs the floor while I look around. The computer system is just the way I left it last night, there's nothing under the recliner, Mom's puppet magazines are piled on the end table as usual, and I don't see any toes sticking out from behind the couch.

"Okay, dog. Help me. Where did you put Iris?"

Nose sits down, tilts his head, and stares at my hands.

"No, I don't have a treat for you. Where's Grandma's leg?"

He dips down, slides his front legs forward, stretches out his long body, then rolls over on his back to look at me upside down.

"Oh, please, I know you have more energy than that." I clap my hands and try to act excited. "Hurry up, boy! Bring me Iris."

He whirls to his feet, throws back his head, gives a short howl, and then runs off to my bedroom. In a few seconds, he returns with his squeaky red ball, drops it at my feet, and then prances around playfully, begging me to throw it.

"This is the last throw until we find Iris," I say as I toss his ball toward the front door. It's a little slimy, though, so it slips out in the wrong direction. I'm glad Mom's not here to see it land on the living room couch.

With a happy yip, Nose bolts up to retrieve it, but when he hops down, his collar snags the multicolored afghan that's piled on one end. It follows him like a rainbow sweeping across the floor, exposing Grandma's leg, there on the couch. It was never stolen at all. She must have forgotten that she covered it during her nap, no doubt confused by the hypoglycemia and maybe the pain pill, too.

The phone rings just as I'm about to announce the good news, so I wait, listening, as Grandma pushes my computer chair over to the wall phone in the kitchen.

"Hello?" she shouts. "What? Roland? Did you say you want to speak to Roland? Just a minute, sweetheart. He's looking for my leg."

Then she hollers into the living room, loud enough to rattle all the windows up and down Western Reserve Avenue. "Yoo hoo, Roland! You're wanted on the telephone! Hurry! It sounds like a sweet little GIRL!"

"Roland? It's me."

"Oh. Hi."

"You know that big math test I asked you to help me study for?"

"Ahhh – no."

Chapter 9

"We talked about it in the *library* this morning?"

"Oh, *that* math test. What about it?"

"Can you meet me at school at seven tonight to work on it?"

"Yeah, I guess."

"Okay. See you then."

That was two hours ago. Since then, I finished my homework, checked my blood sugar, injected my usual insulin dose, and then killed an hour pacing around my room like some kind of lunatic, practicing how to talk to Crystal. Now it's 6:30, only a half hour away from when I'm supposed to meet her, and Mom, with our only car and my only way to get to school, is just getting home. She staggers in with four canvas bags dangling from her shoulders, her foggy glasses teetering on the tip of her nose, and her face radiating lots of energy, like she'll pop if she doesn't tell us her good news right away.

"Guess what?" she gushes. "Someone from Cleveland City Hospital was at the printer's when I was picking up my new brochure and when she saw the photo of our new stump puppet, she jumped at the chance to schedule us for eight shows, starting in January. Plus she wants to hire us to perform at a diabetes fund-raising banquet in March. Not bad for one little errand, huh?"

"Zinnia, do you really think we're ready for eight shows?" asks Grandma, dropping her soup spoon with surprise.

"If we've performed one, we can perform a hundred. You're not getting cold feet, are you, Mother?"

"Well, maybe *one* cold foot." Grandma chuckles and winks at me.

Mom's so excited, she doesn't even notice Grandma's little joke or the fact that we didn't save her any garlic wafers or turkey stew.

"While I was stuck in traffic on my way home," she says, tossing mangoes and tofu into the fridge, "I was thinking about how we need to upgrade our staging. The holidays might get in the way, but I think we'll be ready by January. I'll have to make a list of new materials..."

She closes the fridge and transfers a second bag over to the pantry, pulling out jumbo cans of refried beans, one after the other. My eyes bug out when she reaches for the fifth one.

"Whoa. Did you buy every bean in the whole store?"

Her back stiffens as she slowly turns toward me. She might have noticed me earlier but she didn't really *see* me until now.

"Not quite, but I *should* have since they're half price today. And yes, I used your coupon, Mother." Then her eyes narrow as her instinctual maternal radar switches on. "Did anything *strange* happen this afternoon?"

She aims her question at me first, and then shifts her eyes over to Grandma. Like conspirators, we study our empty soup bowls and keep our mouths shut.

"Well? Did I get any phone calls today?" she asks, a bit louder.

Hoorah, finally a question I feel like answering. "Not since I've been home, but I put your mail on the table."

"Hmm, probably bills. Did you both test and inject on schedule this afternoon?"

We nod, still looking down.

"What about supper? Have you both eaten enough?"

This time, Grandma and I look at each other before nodding again.

"And did you two notice that it's snowing outside?" she asks, returning to her unpacking, apparently satisfied that our diabetes isn't going to kill us during the next few minutes.

"The news is full of warnings about a storm coming from the west, over Lake Erie," says Grandma. "How much snow do we have so far?"

"Hardly any, but the highway was starting to get icy as I got closer to Snowville. As long as the water in Lake Erie is still warm, these early season storms bring us tons of wet, heavy snow. Are you done with your homework, Roland?"

Good, here's the opening I've been waiting for. "Not quite. I should do some group work at school tonight. Can you drive me over?"

My voice must sound suspicious because she suddenly freezes with a can of beans suspended in midair. Turning with a squinty, probing look, she says, "*Group work?* With this bad weather coming?"

Uh oh. It's time to deploy Emergency Rule #3: Never lie to mothers. Unless you *have to,* that is, and this is not one of those *have to* times. I take a deep breath, stop drumming my spoon, and stare directly into her foggy glasses.

"It's just some stuff we didn't finish talking about this morning."

All true.

"And I want to borrow some acting books from the public library," adds Grandma. "Maybe you could drop me off while Roland is at school?"

"You don't need acting books, Mother."

"I know I don't *need* them, Zinnia. But I *want* them. What time are you supposed to be at school, Roland?"

"Seven."

"What?" Mom gasps. "That's only twenty minutes from now. This is pretty short notice, son. When did you find out about this?"

"Today." And then I cinch the deal. "I don't *have* to go. I mean, I *think* I still have straight A's…"

"All right," she grumbles. "We'd better hurry. I'll make a turkey sandwich while you, Roland, get busy clearing those dirty dishes from the table. Are you ready to go, Mother?"

In other words, where's Iris?

"Yes, I'm all attached. Just give me a minute to find my cane and select a hat. I hope my *Frosty the Snowman* cap has fresh batteries."

Nose springs out from behind the family room couch and runs to guard the door. His favorite words, *ready to go,* mean that there's a car ride in his future, and there's no way he's going to miss his chance to go along.

Chapter 10

Crystal is hiding in the shadows by the bus ramp when we get to school a few minutes past seven. She stays undetected thanks to the worsening snowfall and Grandma's noisy struggle to stop Nose from escaping when I open the sliding back door of our rusty mini van.

"Do you have your insulin kit?" Mom shouts over Nose's howling.

"Geez! It's in my book bag, like always. But I won't need it tonight. I'm only going to be here for an hour."

"You never know..." she starts to say before I cut her off by slamming the door. She gives me an irritated look and then drives slowly across the street to the public library. I pause to calm my nerves, and then walk as casually as I can toward Crystal.

"Have you been waiting long?" I ask, noticing the big wet flakes already building up on her ponytail and turquoise ski jacket.

"Not really. Was that your dog I heard barking so loud?"

"Yeah, he wanted to come along. Is the school open?"

"I haven't tried the door. I was afraid I might set off an alarm."

"We won't get in trouble. I've been here lots of times at night." I pull on the handle and rattle the door. "It's locked, all right. Do you see a janitor in there? Or Moonman? He practically lives in the boiler room when he's not driving my bus."

We press our noses against a window, instantly fogging it with Crystal's minty fresh breath and my putrid garlic and turkey mixture.

"I don't see anyone, Roland, but I bet the gym door is open. There's a men's basketball league that plays in there on Monday nights. By the way, do you want some gum?"

"Yeah, okay, as long as it's stronger than garlic..."

She giggles and gives me a piece, so I unwrap it and start to chew as fast as I can while we walk past an old brick smokestack toward the gym entrance on the other side of the school. Then a cloud of toxic smoke blows in and contaminates us both at the same time.

"Eeew! What stinks?" Crystal gasps as she pulls her collar up.

I pinch my nose and peer up at the sparks and soot spewing out of the top of the boiler room chimney. "It's not my breath *this* time. Didn't Moonman announce that he's burning trash now?"

"Yep, my mom says that it's a lot less expensive than fuel oil, but what good is money if we can't breathe? Look at how the smoke makes the snow turn black! How can he get away with polluting like this?"

"Who knows? Maybe people don't care if it keeps taxes down. Let's get out of here."

Crystal's boots slip on an icy patch as we duck away from the fumes. Then she stops to smell her ponytail. "Great. Now my hair stinks like that smoke. I hope my mom doesn't notice. She thinks I'm across the street at the library. My dad gave me a ride and he's going to pick me up around eight."

"We have about an hour then. What's up? I mean, we're not really here about a math test, right?"

She shivers and exhales a long sigh. "We *should* be since math's my worst subject, but I thought we could search the lunchroom for clues about the man who delivered the stolen food to my house."

Standing together like this for the first time, I'm surprised to see that she's about four inches taller than me, so I stretch my neck up before talking again.

"I don't get why you need *me* here. The only thing I know about the lunchroom is how to be a target for supersonic long-range French fry missiles."

A fluffy snowflake lands on her eyelash, so she brushes it away before glaring at me suspiciously. "Are you trying to hint around that you don't *want* to help? I thought you liked my mom."

I feel my face getting hot as I stare back, all too aware of how pretty she is, especially out here in the fresh snow, the two of us, alone. Her green eyes narrow impatiently. "Well? Do you or don't you want to help prove that my mom is innocent?"

Even in the faint overhead light of the parking lot, I can see that she's getting upset again, like this morning. "Crystal, it's not that I don't *want* to help you and your mom, it's just that I don't know *why* you think I can do you any good. My mom and grandma know your folks because of growing up in Snowville together, but you and I aren't exactly best friends."

"Don't you understand, Roland? I *can't* ask my friends for help. If their parents find out that my mom was questioned by the police, they'll never be allowed to speak to me again. And anyway, they're always talking about kids behind their backs. The only reason they include me at all is that they like my horses and maybe 'coz I do okay in sports."

"And you're one of the cutest girls in the whole school," I blurt out, and then I'm instantly sorry. Instead of cheering her up, she catches her breath and looks down like she might cry.

"I mean, at least you're not a nerdy piece of string like me. You're good at sports and you look good, too. That's all most kids care about."

"That's the problem. No one knows the *real* me. They think all I am is a basketball player with lots of hair."

"Which isn't too bad. And anyway, you can't help it that you have great hair. You may as well make the best of it. That's Emergency Rule #1, by the way. Make the best use of what you have."

"You have emergency rules?"

"For as long as I can remember. It's like a little voice in my head that tells me what to do."

"Like an early warning system?"

"Yeah, only it doesn't usually work early."

"Are you some kind of boy scout, Roland?"

"You mean like an eager beaver type who's always prepared?" She nods and giggles.

"I signed up for Cub Scouts in first grade, but I didn't fit in."

"So your emergency rules are something you made up?"

I shrug. "I guess. I mean, it's no biggy."

She glances back toward the old smokestack and sighs. "It's so much easier to label people than to figure out who they *really* are."

"Yeah, like you're popular, I'm not..."

She shakes her head sadly. "Getting hung up about what other people think must be a seventh grade thing 'coz I never even noticed anyone's clothes last year, let alone care whether or not they liked mine. I probably shouldn't care now, but I do. Do you think we're getting more and more shallow every year that we get older?"

"Actually, we're more *frozen* than shallow right now," I say as I try to stop a shiver from traveling down my spine. "But then again, there's a high probability that we're frozen *because* we're shallow, like how a puddle freezes faster than Lake Erie? Less depth, less volume..."

"Are you some kind of mathematician, too?" She's grinning now, her silver braces glinting through the falling snow.

I pull my hands up into my jacket sleeves and shuffle my feet for warmth. "More like a meteorologist. Does my head have a snowbank on it like yours?"

"Yep, you're definitely getting that frosty look." Then her smile vanishes as she remembers why we're here. "Before Lake Erie's relative rate of freezing butted into our conversation, you wanted to know why I asked *you* to help. It's easy. Your grades are great and mine are the pits. You're good with computers and I'm a major technophobe. But most of all, Roland, you're not one of those cooler-than-God cliquey types who yaks about everything all over town."

"So you didn't tell fifty other guys about this?"

"Of course not! And I wouldn't have told *you* except that you were in my hiding spot this morning. We hardly know each other, remember?"

"That means that we're meeting here tonight because of pure coincidence. Nothing but random chance."

"Like how I ended up with your grandma's leg at the mall..."

"Great, I thought you forgot about that."

"Who could ever forget holding some stranger's leg? And the trash can rolling in? That Hawaiian-music-dancing-sunflower-hat thingy? It was a riot!"

"Yeah, *real* funny."

"But who cares? I mean, you don't control what she does. It's not like you were selling tickets or anything."

I think of Mom's new stump puppet and make a solemn pledge to NEVER help with ticket sales.

"Anyway," she adds, "if your grandma didn't pass her leg around, I wouldn't have known about your grades. I mean, who actually *reads* the honor roll?"

I shake my head. "Only the guys I eat lunch with."

She grins. "There is *one* thing I was wondering, Roland. It's none of my business, but does she ever actually *wear* her leg?"

I chuckle, thinking of the wild scene at home this afternoon.

"She said you were looking for it when I called you today."

Embarrassed, I start laughing so hard the snow falls off my head, and then Crystal starts in, too. We look like we're transmitting goofy smoke signals as each chuckle sends a puffy white vapor cloud up into the falling snow.

"What's so funny?" she finally says, catching her breath.

"You wouldn't believe some of the stuff my grandma does."

"It might make you feel better to know that her fake leg isn't nearly as bad as *my* grandpa's dentures. Remember? That's why I noticed the delivery guy's teeth? After my grandma died from a heart attack, my mom started inviting him to everything. He practically lives with us, and even though I beg him not to, he always takes out his chompers and passes 'em around whenever I have friends over."

"Just like my grandma."

"Not quite, 'coz his false teeth have spit and half-chewed food in 'em, like goopy raisins and spinach and other smelly stuff. It's the grossest thing I've ever seen. Once he took 'em out just as I was about to blow out my birthday candles."

"Does he make his teeth tell jokes or stories like a puppet?"

She laughs and shakes her head. "Are you kidding? I'd never let him get *that* far. Whenever he goes for his teeth, I take everyone out to go riding for the rest of the day. Our horses hate my grandpa. Our barn cats do, too. They seem to know he's not an animal lover."

"He's pretty bad, Crystal, but not as bad as my grandma."

"Is too."

"Is not."

"Is *too*," she shouts. "My grandpa's teeth are *much* worse than your grandma's leg!"

I look around. "Tell the whole world, why don't you?"

"No one heard me, Roland. Anyway, it's true."

"Okay, you win, but only because my grandma's leg doesn't have slimy gunk on it. Unless, you smeared some on the other night…"

She slugs my shoulder with a gloved fist, so I fly backwards, pretending that she's really hit me hard. We laugh and start to walk toward the gym again. It's kind of amazing, but this might be the most fun that I've ever had. She's incredibly easy to talk to.

"You don't have to come," she says, serious again. "I'll go in alone."

"Maybe we shouldn't snoop around in there. We don't have much time."

"I *have* to do something. It's all my fault – Hey, do you see those boxes next to the door? They look like they're from the lunchroom."

I go over and brush the snow off a bundle of thick, flattened cardboard. The outside layer is soggy, so this pile must have been here for a while.

"Maybe Moonman forgot to take this inside. He goes around the whole town collecting stuff to burn."

"No, read the labels," she says. "Snowville Middle School Food Service."

I shrug and point at a pop can wedged in the door, which is propped open just enough for us to hear bouncing balls and squeaky shoes coming from the gym.

"You're right about this entrance being open, Crystal. We can sneak in here. It looks like they might be expecting more players to show up."

"Let's hurry before anyone sees us," she whispers.

"Can we get through the gym without messing up their game?"

"Yep, all we have to do is run in like we own the place, steal their ball, dribble down the court, fake out a couple defenders, and then slam-dunk the ball on our way out the other side of the gym."

"Easier said than done," I mutter, imagining myself tripping and getting trampled by a team of sweaty seven-footers chasing Crystal as she runs away with their basketball. But instead of interrupting their game, Crystal grabs a strap of my book bag and yanks me through an unmarked door that veers off to the left of the entrance.

I can't believe it! Is this a nightmare or a dream come true? She's pulling me into the girl's locker room!

"Close your eyes," snickers Crystal. "I don't want to shatter your adolescent male fantasies about this place."

I'm so jittery, I forget to look around as she grabs my elbow and rushes me over

Chapter 11

a dirty cement floor past battered blue lockers, drippy shower stalls, and crusty metal benches. In just a couple seconds, she escorts me around a corner, opens a windowless door, and presto! We've totally bypassed the gym and pop out in the school's main hallway. I know I shouldn't let her get away with that adolescent male fantasy wisecrack, but I'm too stunned by this momentous historical event to think of anything to say.

I, Roland W. Weedervich, being almost twelve and of sound mind and body, on this, the first Monday night after Thanksgiving, HAVE JUST TOURED THE GIRLS LOCKER ROOM!!! I glance down at my wet shoes. Yes! My footprints are still there! Warthog will hoot about this!

Crystal doesn't even notice that something earth-shattering has just happened. She releases me, pulls off her gloves, stuffs them in her pockets, and starts to march down the shadowy hallway with a long, determined-looking stride, exactly like a girl on a serious mission. I have to jog just to keep up.

The overhead florescent lighting is always dim in this old building, but now the hallway looks especially murky, like an out-of-focus scene in a scary movie. Everything seems exaggerated, too. The ceiling looms higher than usual, normally hidden patterns leap out from the tiled floor, and the yellow brick walls seem energized, as if on guard against intruders. Even the smell is fortified. Sixty years of chalk dust and old books have combined with moldy boots, sweaty gym uniforms, and ammonia sulfate science experiments, giving Snowville Middle School a very distinctive aroma.

In other words, the place *stinks*.

It must have something to do with Moonman's new heating system because I don't remember it ever smelling this bad during the day. As we hurry away from the gym, I hear the steady hum of a vacuum cleaner up ahead.

"Crystal? Someone must be cleaning the Regurge-a-Dirge Factory."

"Yep, it's the only carpeted room in the whole school. Let's be extra quiet when we get close since it's across from the lunchroom."

I'm definitely getting the creeps, but Crystal seems unaffected by the spooky hallway.

"My mom told me some more about what the police said," she whispers, slowing down a bit to let me catch up. "They kept asking her about inventory records and this thick stack of computer printouts."

"Were the printouts from here?"

She shrugs. "I guess so, and from the superintendent's office, too. And it turns out that they haven't formally charged her with anything, but the school food they found at our house makes her the main suspect. That's why the superintendent doesn't want her working right now."

"Shhh," I whisper, reminding her about the vacuumer. She nods and we tiptoe the rest of the way. My mind is still back on the computer printouts as we push the lunchroom door open and sneak inside. It's so dark, we have to grope around until we bump into something hard. I drop my book bag and shudder at the racket it makes. Then, as my eyes adjust, I begin to make out the outline of chairs stacked upside down on long wooden tables. We each pull one off the table and sit down. The door is still ajar, so a small patch of light seeps in from the hallway. At least we'll be able to find our way out.

"Do you think we should turn on the lights?" asks Crystal. "I can't even see your face."

"No, not unless we have to. We shouldn't risk being seen. Crystal, back to what you were saying about the printouts – is all the food that gets delivered entered into the computer records?"

"Yep, that's what my mom calls the inventory. Our school got a new computer last spring so she had to work on entering information all summer. She had to type in usage records, too."

"What's that?"

"It's everything the lunchroom uses, I guess. You know, all the containers of food that are opened and dumped into recipes. All the cleaning supplies, too. The Central Office, where the superintendent works, wanted to find out if there were patterns of usage over the last five years so they could save money in their ordering. The other Snowville schools had to enter their records, too."

"So both of the elementary schools, the middle school, and the high school all got the new computer system and they all had to enter in all the food and supplies that were bought and used during the last five years?"

"Right, and then the Central Office person who pays for everything entered in the payment records for the same five years. When everything was compared, it turned out that the schools were paying for lots more food than was getting used in school lunches. The food was getting checked in and approved, but then some of it was disappearing. They figured it was stolen."

"Was it disappearing at all the schools?"

"I don't know. My mom only knows about the middle school."

"Who checked in and approved the deliveries at our school?"

"My mom. That's why she's in such big trouble. Plus the evidence the police found at our house."

"Crystal, isn't it weird that the police knew that the food was in your freezer and under the sink?"

"It sure is. Only two people knew where it was."

"You and the toothless skeleton guy."

"He had some teeth."

"Okay, but is it possible that someone else saw the food? Do you hire anyone to clean your house or work at your stables?"

"You're right, Roland! I forgot that we had so much company on Thanksgiving. Both my sisters were home from college and my grandpa was there, of course, and my Aunt Rose and Uncle Tom from Akron, and their four boys, and then my Grandma Nellson came later – you know, she's the one I mentioned at the mall? My grandma who hates leaving Snowville? And let's see, there was – Oh, no! Grandma Nellson's sister, my dad's Aunt Eunice, went out to the freezer to get ice cream and she was poking around under the sink, too. She said she was looking for dish soap."

"Why would your Great Aunt Eunice tattle on your mom?"

"She wouldn't do it on purpose, but she talks nonstop. Maybe she made a joke about our turkey tasting as bad as those orange light bulb chicken things. And she's mean enough to think that our mashed potatoes were made from those dried flakes under the sink. She's got a sick sense of humor and a really loud, annoying voice."

"So if a Snowville cop who was already working on the case of the missing food happened to overhear your Great Aunt Eunice…"

"Right. All a cop would have to do is ask her one question and she'd tell him more than he ever wanted to know. Should I call her tonight and find out where she went last Friday and Saturday?"

"Maybe you should wait until tomorrow. I mean, can you stand more torture today?"

She giggles. "Good point. Anyway, even if we've figured out how the police knew where to look for the school food, we still aren't any closer to finding the delivery guy. He could have been the one who told the police where the food was."

"Why would he?"

"He might want to get my mom in trouble. You know, make her look guilty."

"Do you think the delivery guy is violent? He could be an escaped convict or maybe even a murderer. I bet his teeth got punched out in prison or while he was attacking someone. And he knows exactly where you live, Crystal. Do you think he might try to shut you up before you talk to the police anymore?"

She's quiet for a few moments and her voice is tense when she finally answers. "I've messed up big time, haven't I? I've been thinking about all the wrong things! Half the time I've been feeling guilty about causing trouble for my mom and the other half, I've been worrying about what kids at school are going to say when they find out. What I *should* have been focusing on is the fact that I saw the guy with the stolen food."

"You're a witness to a crime!"

"Possibly the only witness."

"But think about this, Crystal. Why would the delivery guy march right up to you in the middle of the day?"

"Maybe he wanted to be sneakier, but couldn't because I was in the driveway all afternoon. Or he might have been afraid that my mom and dad were coming home pretty soon. He could have been desperate to plant the evidence at my house."

"Or off his rocker. Did seem upset?"

"No, not really. When he said that my mom would know what to do with the food, he seemed like a regular guy. His missing teeth made him look odd and he was real skinny and pale, but he wasn't mean or crazy-acting. Maybe he was just making a delivery for someone else and didn't realize that it was illegal."

"That could explain why he didn't mind being seen."

"Unless he was counting on people not believing me. Because that's exactly what's happened. I don't think my mom even believes me. Everyone treats me like a little kid."

"Maybe he was just planning to eliminate you later."

"Eliminate me?"

"Yeah, you know, rub you out so you can't testify against him."

"You've seen too many gangster movies, Roland. Stuff like that doesn't happen in Snowville."

"We're only twelve miles from Cleveland. Aren't there over two million people around here? A few of them must be criminals."

"Probably a lot more than a few."

"What if this missing food problem is happening to other schools in other suburbs, too? You said it amounted to $10,000 here. What if the food wasn't really stolen? Maybe it's some kind of scheme where a company charges schools for more food than it delivered? Wouldn't that add up to tons of money?"

"Yep, this could be some kind of organized crime."

"Do you think that guy followed you here tonight?"

"Roland, you're scaring me."

"Seriously, Crystal. Did you see a white pickup truck out there?"

"It's snowing, remember? They all looked white."

"You'd better watch out. And meanwhile, if we can find some way of proving to the police that your mom isn't involved, then the pressure will be off of you, too. There must be clues somewhere in those computer printouts."

Instead of answering, Crystal starts to make squirmy noises. Her chair scrapes against the floor, her ski jacket rustles, she drops something, probably a glove, and then she blows her nose. I hope she's not crying again, like this morning. I'm starting to feel restless, too, so I stand up to stretch.

"Are you leaving, Roland?"

"No, but I don't see how sitting in a dark lunchroom is helping your mom at all. We have to find the delivery guy and the only way that's going to happen here at school is if he's standing right out there in the hallway, ready to pounce."

"It might help if we search my mom's office. It's behind the kitchen area. You could check her computer while I go through the storage rooms. Maybe the food isn't missing at all. It could be covered up, or stuffed away in a closet."

"That's a good idea, but don't you think the police already looked everywhere?"

"What if they didn't look good enough?"

"Isn't your mom's office locked at night? Going in there would definitely set off alarms."

"I have her new set of keys."

"What? Are you sure she didn't send you in here to get something?"

"No way. I'd be grounded forever if she found out I took her keys."

Crystal clutches the sleeve of my jacket and starts to beg, "Come on, Roland. Help me. Please! I'm no good with computers at all."

"I don't think I should go in there, Crystal. I mean, you're related to the lunchroom manager. You sortta belong. But I'd get worse than grounded if we got caught. More like ground up."

"But I don't know what to do."

"Can't you turn on her computer and open a few files?"

"Open files?" she asks, genuinely puzzled.

"Yeah, you know, point and click…"

"Roland, when you have horses, you don't even have time to watch TV, let alone mess around with computers. I practically flunked Computer Lab last year, and anyway, even if I wanted to use our iMac, my dad has it all bogged down with his business records. There's barely enough memory on it for me to do my history reports."

"So you don't surf the web or send E-mail? No Instant Messaging?"

"I don't care about any of that stuff. Come on, Roland, it must be close to eight o'clock already. If we're going to look at her computer, we'd better…"

"Wait! Listen!"

I hear footsteps approaching in the hallway. They sound heavy. Hesitant. Then they stop by the lunchroom door. Is the delivery guy coming after Crystal already?

"Let's hide!" she hisses.

"No! We're trapped in here! We have to get out!"

We dash for the door, but just as we burst out into the hallway, *smack!* I run into someone wearing a black uniform, a gun, and a shiny gold badge.

And a frown.

A very suspicious frown.

Chapter 12

My zipper digs into my throat as Brad Copper, the officer assigned to teach our antidrug program, grabs my jacket collar from behind. He was a star lineman for the Snowville Blizzards and I'm expecting him to use me as a tackling dummy any second now.

"Whoa! What's your rush?" he says, as he lets go and shoves me just hard enough to knock me off balance.

"Oh, hi," I sputter, trying my hardest to look cooperative. "Sorry I ran into you, sir. I didn't see you lurking…"

"Me? Lurking? What were you two doing in there?"

As usual, I don't know what to say. Will he believe that we were just talking? Crystal nudges my foot, but I'm afraid to look at her.

"Answer me. *Now*."

Just as my knobby knees start to cave in, Crystal comes to my rescue by pushing my shoulder and saying, "See, Toadface? I *told* you not to throw my glove in there."

Officer Copper's frown relaxes as he crosses his bulging arms and rolls his electric blue eyes upward. "Did you lose something, Miss?"

"Not exactly. I can't find my glove after *someone* threw it in the lunchroom." She sticks out her lower lip, puts her hands on her hips, and taps her boot impatiently. An award-winning performance if I've ever seen one.

"A guy has to defend himself somehow," I mumble, trying to follow her lead. "Did you hear what she called me, Mr. Copper? It's a good thing you came along. Who knows what she'd do next?"

"I'm not getting in the middle of *this* nonsense," he mutters, shaking his head. "Let me see if I can find the light switch."

We step aside and make scared faces at each other while he feels the wall next to the lunchroom door. The lights buzz and then flick on.

"Well, looky here. One blue glove on the floor, two chairs down from the table, and what's that? A plain black book bag?" He pats his nightstick and rocks back and forth while his calculating eyes study our faces. "Hmm, we have incriminating evidence left behind by two guilty-looking juveniles running from a dark room in a locked school that's not supposed to have anyone in it beyond the gymnasium."

I ignore him and hustle in to get the glove. "Here's your precious little mitty, Bubblebrain! Are you happy now?"

"Not as long as you're alive, Sewerbreath," she pouts, while I nervously set the chairs back up on the table and retrieve my book bag. Mr. Copper doesn't look as mad when I return to the hallway, but he's not exactly buying our little spat, either. He rubs his blond crew cut as he watches me, puzzled. Then his eyes light up.

"I finally figured out where I've seen you before. You're Sophie Zollo's grandson. What's your name again?"

"Roland."

"Oh, yeah. It's Weedsomething, isn't it?"

"Weedervich."

"That's right. You're the kid who let the beagle puppy destroy those raspberries last summer."

"I didn't exactly *let* him do it. I mean, it was an accident."

I wouldn't look at Crystal right now if you paid me a million bucks. The mountainous policeman makes a deep, gargling noise that might be a chuckle. Or a grunt.

"Your mom used to baby-sit for my brother and me every Tuesday night when my folks went bowling," he says, almost friendly. "She came up with awesome ideas for how to turn junk into toys."

"That sounds like her."

"Is she picking you up tonight?"

"Yes, sir."

"Tell her little Bradley says hi."

"*Little* Bradley?" Crystal and I look at each other and snicker.

"Yeah, she used to call me that, even after I got to be *this* size. You don't mind me looking inside that book bag of yours, do you?"

"Mind? Yes, sir, I sortta do," I say, thinking of my diabetes kit.

"Do you have a search warrant?"

There I go, sticking my foot in my mouth just when we're starting to get along. He steps forward and pokes my shoulder.

"I don't need a warrant for searching a trespasser's book bag on school property," he says forcefully. "Maybe you'd rather show it to me down at the station where we'll haul you both in for breaking and entering..."

"*Okay*, it's no biggy. Look all you want," I mutter, handing it over.

He unzips the large middle section and examines my books and pencil case, but when he opens the smaller front pocket, my diabetes kit clatters to the floor.

"What's this? A syringe? You have drugs at school?"

"Look at the label! It's insulin, okay? As in a necessary lifesaving prescription?"

"Are you getting smart with me, Mr. Weedervich?" he sneers, his bristly chin jutting out stubbornly.

I exhale and look at the floor. "No, sir. Just put it back, please. The way this night is going, I might be needing it pretty soon."

His icy blue eyes keep drilling into me until he finally says, "Diabetic, huh? I need more proof. Where's your medic alert ID?"

I sigh and pull a gold chain out from under my shirt. He quickly scans the tag, then closes my kit and puts it back in my book bag. This time I keep my big mouth shut, so he shifts his attention over to Crystal.

"Aren't you Opal Nellson's daughter?"

She looks at me and nods, her angelic green eyes starting to brim with tears. "How do you know me?"

"My niece, Sarah, played on your basketball team last year so I went to a few of your games. Snowville's changing, but it's still small enough to keep track of most folks, especially the families that have lived here a while. And talk about keeping track of folks, what were you two *really* doing in the lunchroom tonight? And I don't want to hear more baloney about a glove fight."

Just like that, he's glaring and frowning again, pulling off the good-cop, bad-cop routine all by himself.

Crystal starts to whimper, "We were just…"

"Don't tell him," I say, jabbing her with my elbow.

"Tell me what?" he thunders, turning toward me.

"Um, you know, Crystal. The surprise?"

There I go. A lie. I must have lost my mind. Too bad I don't have an emergency rule for how to deal with angry policemen.

"But we got caught, so it's not a surprise anymore," she sputters, her eyes wide with confusion. "So, um – *surprise* – Yep, I was thinking it might be fun to have a surprise party for the girl's seventh grade basketball team. You know, to get the season off to a…"

"Nice try, Crystal," interrupts Mr. Copper coldly. "I know all about your mom's troubles. As the school liaison officer, I've been working on the case of the stolen food since October."

Crystal coughs like she's just been punched in the stomach. "Then you must know that she's totally innocent!"

"As a matter of fact, I know nothing of the sort." Then he turns to me and growls, "You'd better be running along home now, Mr. Weedervich."

"Nooo," whines Crystal. She grabs my hand. "He's helping me."

Officer Copper snorts. "Oh, really? What did you call him before? Toadface? Sewerbreath? Some friend you are."

She covers her face with her other hand and sniffs. I desperately want to snatch mine back, but she's practically squeezing it off.

"Here's what I think is going on," he says, his voice low and gritty. "I think you two know something about the stolen food situation and you came here tonight to tamper with evidence."

"No, sir." My stomach flips when I hear how wimpy I sound.

"No? Then you had better start convincing me otherwise."

I squash Crystal's hand for good luck and take a deep breath to steady myself. "Crystal just wanted to tell me about the thug who brought the school food to her house. We thought we'd be able to think of why he did it."

"While returning to the scene of the crime?"

"No, we just went in there to get away from the snow and the basketball players." Crystal lets go of my hand and starts digging in her pocket, dumping her glove out again.

I pick it up and go on with what I hope sounds like a good explanation. "We think that some company has been cheating the school and getting away with it because they deliver to one place and send the bill to another. Mrs. Nellson doesn't get the bill, so she can't confirm that it's right, and the Central Office lady doesn't see the food, so she doesn't know how much was really delivered.

"No one found out about the cheating until we got the new computer system. We think that the food wasn't stolen at all. It was just never delivered in the right amounts in the first place. The cheaters probably came during a time when Mrs. Nellson was too busy to count every little thing, like in the middle of lunch. And then when the computer caught up with them, they planted phony evidence against her to make her look guilty. The only thing she ever did wrong was to be too nice and too busy."

"It's not a crime to be nice and busy," adds Crystal. "You don't really think she stole from the school, do you?"

"What I think doesn't matter. It's the evidence that counts. You kids shouldn't be getting mixed up in this."

"But I'm already involved," says Crystal. "I saw the *real* thief."

"Yeah, and that creep might want to hurt her."

"Have you been threatened?" he asks sternly.

"Well, no…"

"Followed?"

"No."

"Do you get strange hang-up phone calls at home?"

"Yes, sir. We get lots of those."

"So do we," I add.

"And so does every Snowville resident. That's one of the aggravations of living in an upscale suburb like this. Every computerized telemarketer in the country targets our phones. But Crystal, have you had unusual calls where someone might be trying to find out if you're home alone?"

"I don't think so," she admits.

"So, it doesn't sound like you're in any danger from your mom's accomplice."

"Accomplice? Do you think that icky man is someone my mom would have as a partner?"

"It looks that way to us," he says, "*if* he exists at all, that is."

"Have you checked the other schools for missing food?" I ask.

"Of course."

"And other towns?"

"Yes, we're checking all aspects of the case. The stealing doesn't appear to be widespread, but other school districts don't have our new computer system, so it takes longer to spot a problem like this."

"Did you tell them about the white pickup truck, Crystal?"

She nods. "And the brown uniform."

"What was the license number on the vehicle?" he asks, pulling out a well-worn spiral notebook.

Crystal shrugs.

"The make and model?"

"How would I know? I'm only twelve." Her shaky voice fades to nothing, matching the hopelessness in her red-rimmed eyes.

He shuffles his feet impatiently, pockets his notebook, and surveys the hallway. "Your theory might have possibilities, Mr. Weedervich," he mutters. "It'd be easy to check the computer records to see if all the missing food came from just one or two companies. But for now, I want you both to mind your own business and let the authorities handle the investigation."

"Roland is great with computers," says Crystal. "He could…"

"No, thanks. The only time I accept help from juveniles is during Pee Wee football games. And that's only when they're playing or officiating."

He pauses and looks me up and down, mentally weighing my meager skin and bones. "You weren't out for football this fall, were you Mr. Weedervich?"

"No, sir, but I'd be happy to look through the printouts, maybe..."

"Are your ears full of wax or is your brain a couple doughnuts short of a dozen?" he interrupts, completely drained of patience. "What part of *no* don't you understand? Vacate the premises. *Now.* I'm going to inspect the whole school, especially the lunchroom storage areas. If you told me the truth about staying out of there, you have nothing to worry about."

"We only sat in those chairs," I say. "Come on, Crystal. It's past eight. I bet our rides are outside."

Officer Copper glares at us as we hurry toward the door leading to the bus ramp. Crystal's dad is already there at the curb and Mom and Grandma are just arriving.

"Meet me in the library tomorrow morning," she whispers.

I nod as she gets into her dad's car and drives away. When Mom pulls up next, I glance over at the cars parked near the gym door. Officer Copper's patrol car is next to a pickup truck that suddenly turns on its headlights and follows Crystal out of the parking lot. It's snowing harder than ever and all the cars are covered with at least two inches, but the truck following Crystal is white underneath the snow, too. The driver looks over and scowls at us as he drives by.

"That man's got the boniest face I've ever seen," says Mom. "Did you see him, Roland? He looks like one of my Halloween puppets."

"Like a skeleton," I gasp. "A mean, toothless skeleton." And he's following Crystal! I have to warn her. But how? *Think!*

"Mom? Can we stop at Mel's Stables on the way home? I just realized that the girl who lives there has a notebook I need tonight." I try to sound normal. The last thing I need is Mom getting all hyped up with too much worry.

"Isn't that where Mel and Opal Nellson live, Mother?" she says to Grandma while I try to stop Nose from licking my face off.

"Yes, next to Alfred's farm. We'd better hang onto Nose if we go over there. He said he'd shoot him the next time he got loose."

"So, can we drop by for a second?" I ask again. But my voice is too high-pitched, so I cough a couple times, hoping Mom won't notice the panic that's starting to take me over.

"At this time of night? Without even calling first? Can't you get it tomorrow?"

I take a deep breath and sigh as loudly as I can. "Yeah, okay... I guess missing *one* homework assignment is no biggy..."

"All *right*, Roland, we'll go over there, but buckle your seat belt and keep Nose quiet! The roads have gotten treacherous and we can't have any more trouble because of that little dog."

Chapter 13

Our short detour to Crystal's house is even more of a white-knuckler than my usual trips with Mom. Wild driving's not her problem. She's too careful! Especially the way she stops at yellow lights. She's so cautious, she slows down at *green* lights, afraid that they're about to turn yellow. And when there's ice under fresh snow like now, you have to look out the window just to find out if you're moving at all. It's maddening! Crystal was probably kidnapped decades ago while Mom searched for the safest route out of the middle school parking lot.

Tonight, since we're going to Crystal's house, we have to pass our usual exit and drive farther east on Route 12 to Overlook Road, a half mile out of our way. The Snowville U-Pick-M Raspberry Farm is there at that intersection, and Mel's Stables is next door. Then just a little farther down Overlook, our street, Western Reserve Avenue, exits off to the left and loops through a bunch of older neighborhoods, eventually winding back to Route 12.

Even though I've lived in Snowville practically my whole life, it's still amazing how quickly snow dumps down on Northern Ohio whenever cold air hits the warmer, open water of Lake Erie. Route 12 was wet when we left home tonight, but now, only an hour later, it looks like a wide, ungroomed ski slope. It's snowing so hard I can barely make out Crystal's tire tracks ahead of us.

Grandma and I know better than to distract Mom in bad weather, but Nose has a special talent for picking times like this to show off his bratty side. Maybe he senses my nervousness, because he's even more annoying than usual. After I stop him from licking my face off, he tries to bite the little handle on my jacket zipper. When he gives up on that, he nuzzles my chest and jams his cold nose in my armpit. I yank him out of there, so he gets back at me by diving into the rear of the van and bellowing out a good one.

"Roland! I told you to keep that dog quiet!"

"I'm trying. But it's impossible."

My seat belt won't let me stretch back far enough to grab his collar, so he's free to tunnel under the back seat, spring over my shoulder, and come stumbling into my lap, yipping and yelping all the way. But before he can leap toward Grandma in the front, I hug him so tight that even his cold nose won't let him escape again.

Meanwhile, Mom is squinting through a tiny slit in the windshield while the wipers battle with the falling snow. The defroster is going full blast and Grandma keeps turning around to yell things like, 'What's all that scuffling back there?' Instead, she should be thanking me for saving her from an airborne beagle attack.

By the time we finally approach our left turn onto Overlook Road, Mom is driving too slow to make it through the intersection. We get stuck in the middle of the road, our tires spinning in place, until a scary look of determination crosses her face. That's when she tightens her grip on the steering wheel, takes a deep breath, and guns it.

Before I can say 'Way to go, Mom!' we shoot forward onto a hidden patch of ice and slide out of control, spinning around in a complete circle before slipping to the left onto Overlook Road. Just as we make the turn, we catch more ice, skid past the U-Pick-M place, fishtail off to the right, and BAM! We smash into a white pickup truck that's stopped in the road next to Crystal's driveway.

As soon as we pile into the truck, a bunch of different things happen at the same time. On impact, Mom screams, Nose howls, and in an automatic reflex to brace myself, I throw my arms forward, releasing Nose to complete his original mission of pouncing Grandma. He sails off into Grandma's lap, making her scream, too. When Mom hears Grandma, she hollers again. And while all this is going on inside our van, the back tailgate of the white pickup truck unlatches. Two metal traps and a big cardboard box tumble out onto the hood of our van, scattering small tan things out across the snow.

Mom stops screaming and turns off the motor. "Is anyone hurt?" she gasps, looking at Grandma and me, her eyes wide with fear.

Before I can answer, the truck driver slams his door and stomps toward us. He's wearing a black stocking cap and camouflage hunting clothes, and in the unnatural brightness of our headlights, his pale face looks thinner than ever. His beady eyes glint with rage when he sees that our front bumper has dented his back fender. He pounds his fist on our van and then winds up and punches his box all the way down into the ditch below the road.

Even Nose is shocked into silence. Mom whispers, "What should I do now?"

Before I can tell her to run for her life, she does the worst possible thing. She rolls down her window! Nose sees his golden opportunity, wiggles away from Grandma, crosses to Mom's side, and squeezes out before anyone can stop him. I've never seen him act so fierce! He lands in front of our van, bares his teeth, and snarls as though he weighs an extra hundred pounds. With his back fur up in a menacing ridge, he lowers his head and starts to whirl around the man, darting in to bite his pants every other second or so. He's moving so fast he looks like a whole army of beagles. I hope the guy's wearing decent underwear because I can see right off that his pants don't stand a chance.

"Stop him, Roland," Mom shouts. "I've caused an accident and now I'll be charged with having a dangerous dog, too!"

I leap out to catch Nose, but the ice is too slick and I crash down, landing flat on my butt next to the door. When I try to pull myself up, I slip again and end up falling into the ditch, crushing the man's cardboard box even worse. Nose circles down to lick my face, then howls nonstop on his way back up for his next attack.

"Get that dog away from me!" the driver barks as he tries to kick Nose. But each time he swings his boot, Nose ducks and veers away.

Just as I struggle out of the ditch, Nose discovers the small tan things that spilled out earlier. I don't know what they are, but they're perfect beagle bait. He takes a mouthful, whips back around toward the driver, avoids a kick, goes in for a quick rip, and returns again for another taste. Meanwhile, Mom gets out of the van.

"I'm sorry…" she starts to say, but is interrupted by Nose zipping by for another raid. She tries to block him, but he swerves and nearly knocks her over as the man aims his boot again.

"Don't kick him," she shouts.

"Get control of your dog, lady!" His voice is hoarse and mean.

"Leave him alone! He won't hurt you unless you hurt him."

"I'm not taking that chance, lady. Get him away from me!"

I guess Mom doesn't like his tone, because she suddenly loses it. "Look what you did to my van!" she hollers. "Those metal traps of yours scratched the hood and look, the bumper is ruined!"

She's waving her arms, he's shaking his fist, Nose is howling, Grandma's banging on the window, snow is flying, and I'm expecting a brawl to break out any second.

"What do you mean, what I've done? *You* hit *me!*"

"You asked for it, parked in the middle of the road like that! I didn't even see your white truck in all this snow. You should have left your headlights on. Don't you know how icy it is?"

"And don't you know how fast a battery wears down when you leave your lights on in this kind of weather? I'm stuck, lady, not parked. I was just trying to get home, when you and your good-for-nothing rust bucket came along and rear-ended me. I'm lucky you didn't – OUCH! Control of that dog or I'll shoot it right now!"

I look into the cab of his truck and see a rifle mounted on the back window. I whistle for Nose, but he ignores me and snatches off an extra-long piece of the driver's pants. That leaves me with only option. Nose can never resist a chase, so if I run away, maybe he'll follow. I take a few clumsy steps toward Crystal's driveway and clap my frozen hands. "Come on, boy! Let's go for a run!"

Nose stops and looks at me, cocking his head back and forth. He decides not to follow, and instead, starts to eat the small tan stuff as fast as he can. He's not under control yet, but at least he's stopped howling and shredding the man's pants.

"Run to the Nellson house, Roland!" shouts Mom. "Tell them to call the police!"

"No! Wait!" the man yells as he cautiously backs away. "Try to get your dog now, lady. You can grab him from behind."

Mom and I look at each other and nod. She steps over the metal traps and sneaks up behind Nose while I approach him from the front. He peeks up at me, but he's too greedy to stop eating. One more gulp gives Mom the millisecond she needs to grab his tail. He tries to pull away, but she reels him in, scoops him up, and hands him off to me.

"Put him in the van and make sure he stays there," she says, her voice still angry.

I carry him over to Grandma's open door. "Did you shut Mom's window?" I ask, afraid to put him down.

She nods, so I toss Nose inside and tell him to stay, as though, ha, ha, he's really going to listen. He burps real loud, shakes off the snow, and curls up in Grandma's lap, just like nothing's wrong. By the time I step back to the front of our van, the man has already packed up both traps and he's trying to cram what's left of the cardboard box inside, too. But the wind is blowing so hard, I can hardly hear what he's saying.

"...to involve the police. This old rattletrap... so we don't need to... I'll go ahead and..."

"My old van is on its last leg, too," Mom says as I lean in closer.

"All right, then. Try not to hit anyone else tonight," he snarls as he slams his tailgate and scowls again at the dent we made in his bumper.

"Watch out, Roland. We have to get out of the way. He's going to try to get started by pushing off from our van. Once he's gone, we should be able to drive forward, too."

Back inside, our windows are so foggy and snowy, I can't see out at all. We hear the truck roar, and as our windshield wipers swipe feebly at the snow, fumes pour out of the truck as it nudges us back before suddenly lurching forward, its rear tires spinning and weaving as it slips away down Overlook Road.

"Did you get his license number, Mom?"

She just sits there shivering, letting her glasses fog up, refusing to answer.

"His name is enough, Roland," says Grandma. "He lives in Snowville, doesn't he, Zinnia?"

Her only response is a bunch of deep breaths. We wait a few seconds until I can't stand it anymore. "You got his *name*, didn't you?" I say, louder than I should.

Mom still won't say anything.

"You have to report this, you know," says Grandma, getting cross.

Mom groans and then thumps her forehead with frustration. "How could I be so stupid?" she mutters, tearing off her glasses and wiping them on her coat. "I don't have the slightest idea who he is. It all happened so fast, and with Nose loose, and all the snow…"

"What? You didn't get his name? What if he comes after us? He has a gun!"

"Settle down, Roland. He said he doesn't want to involve the police, that his old truck isn't worth the paperwork."

"What about Nose? Did he say anything about reporting him?"

She shakes her head, her eyes getting misty.

"Did Nose bite him, or just his pants?" I persist.

"I don't know," Mom sputters. "His pants were torn but he didn't say anything about getting bit. He was pretty mad, though."

"Did he get *your* name?" My voice is trembling now.

"No, and he didn't ask for my license, either."

"What about our front license plate? Did he see it?"

"Go out and see if it's visible, son. And find a piece of whatever Nose was eating. We need to know if it's going to make him sick."

I shiver from both fear and cold as I trudge out to the front of our van and see that our license plate is perfectly clear and easy to read. How long will it be before he traces it and starts stalking us, too?

My fingers are already frozen, so feeling around in the snow for small tan things is not exactly what I want to do right now. I find one right away where we captured Nose. When I hold it up to the headlights, I can hardly believe my eyes! It's part of a veggie paddy, like the kind we had for lunch at school today. I put it in my pocket and hurry back to the van just in time to hear Grandma arguing with Mom.

"But Zinnia, dear, don't you *have* to make a police report in order to collect the insurance money we'll need to get the van fixed?"

Mom shakes her head with frustration. "I don't *know*, Mother! I've never filed a car insurance claim before."

"Well, we'd better get out of here before someone slips into us, too," says Grandma, shifting Nose at bit. He hasn't moved or made a sound since snuggling in her lap.

Mom nods decisively. "All right. This is what we'll do. Roland? You have to get a notebook from your classmate, right?"

"Yeah…"

"Okay. You get out and walk over there. I'll try to get us moving again. If we don't come to pick you up in a minute or two, ask the Nellsons to come out and give us a push. I'll call the police to report the accident when we get home. There's no reason for us to sit out here in the cold anymore tonight. It's times like this that I wish we could afford a cell phone. If the stump puppet gets popular…"

Slogging up to Crystal's front door and asking for a notebook I don't even need seems like a real dumb thing to do. Maybe I can talk Mom into skipping this part so we can just get the heck out of here. I can warn Crystal from home now that the delivery guy is gone.

"Ah, Mom? Don't you think it's a little too late to go over to their house now?"

I guess she doesn't agree, because she pounds her fist on the steering wheel and turns around to glare at me. Before she can chew me out for being the one who insisted on coming this way, I jump back outside, pull my bare hands up into my sleeves, and follow Crystal's tire tracks to a giant horseshoe arch at the entrance of her driveway. That's when I hear a high-pitched howling sound behind me.

It's not Nose this time.

It's a siren.

And it's coming this way.

I don't see any flashing lights, so I keep jogging down Crystal's driveway. It curves sharply to the left around trees so thick and tangled, I can't see any part of her house until I get around the bend. It turns out to be an old farmhouse with

Chapter 14

a wide wraparound porch. All the windows are lit up and when I step closer, security lights turn on in the front yard, too. The tire tracks I've been following enter into a closed garage, so I stop at the front sidewalk where a shovel-width of snow has just been cleared away.

Mr. Nellson shoves his arms into a wooly plaid jacket as he steps out onto the porch. "Who's there?" he shouts.

"It's just me, sir. Roland Weedervich?" I try not to jiggle too much, but it's hard to stand still when my feet feel like ice. "I go to school with Crystal. She lives here, right?"

"She did the last time I looked upstairs. What do you want, son? It's pretty late to be stopping by for a visit."

"I just had a meeting with Crystal at the middle school? And if it's all right with you, I was hoping I could get a notebook from her?"

"You're lucky. We just got home. Don't stand out there on the sidewalk. Come up to the porch and get out of that cold wind."

I walk up the steps just as Mrs. Nellson joins her husband and leans halfway out the door. She's wearing fluffy pink slippers and a bright red bathrobe. It's the first time that I've seen her without her official white apron. The porch light is shining directly in her eyes, so she has to shield them as she looks out at me.

"Roland? Is that you behind that respiration cloud? I hope you didn't walk all the way here in this bad weather."

"No, ma'am, my mom is out on Overlook Road."

"Why didn't she pull in? Is she afraid of getting stuck in our driveway?"

"No, she had a little fender-bender out there. But she thinks she can pick me up in a minute or two."

"Is anyone hurt?"

"No, we're all fine. It was no biggy. Just a couple little dents."

"Does she need help?"

"Only if she can't get started on the ice."

"Oh, my!" she gasps. "Did this happen about five minutes ago?"

"Yes, ma'am."

Her eyes light up as a wide grin spreads across her face. "And there were two vehicles? A mini van and a pickup truck?"

"Uh huh."

She chuckles. "Do you have a beagle with you?"

"Yes, ma'am." I'm wondering what could possibly be so funny about our accident. Mr. Nellson must be thinking the same thing because he keeps giving his wife mean looks and clearing his throat real loud. Then she hugs herself and smiles even bigger.

"Was your dog loose tonight?"

"Yeah, how did you know?" I glance back at Overlook Road, but their trees are so thick, I can't see the road from here.

"Opal? What's going on?" hisses Mr. Nellson, embarrassed.

Mrs. Nellson gestures for us to wait while she bends over, laughing hysterically. That's when Crystal comes to the door.

"Mom, what's so fun… " She looks out at me. "Roland! What are *you* doing here?"

Before I can answer, Mrs. Nellson controls herself enough to say, "You'll never guess what your grandfather did now!"

We all look at each other and smile. We can't help it. Hilarity is contagious, even if it doesn't make sense.

Finally Mrs. Nellson wipes her eyes and catches her breath. "Forgive me, Roland," she says, still grinning. "I guess I must have needed a good laugh. This isn't even that funny."

"Geez, Mom, what's with you?" asks Crystal, annoyed.

She chuckles again. "Grandpa just called to warn us about a big accident up on Overlook. He said a mini van and a pickup truck were both destroyed and that a ferocious hound is on the rampage. He said it sounds exactly like the monster that tore up his raspberries last summer. He loaded his air gun, and he wants us to get armed, too."

Crystal's dad snorts and shakes his head. "That doesn't sound much like Roland's little fender-bender."

"I'm afraid my father embellishes a bit," says Mrs. Nellson.

"He recognized the sound of Roland's dog, though." Crystal says, winking at me.

"That's the part I thought was so funny. You're Sophie Zollo's grandson, aren't you?" she says, grinning at me.

I nod sheepishly, embarrassed by this genetic mishap for the second time tonight.

"Roland, I don't mean to be rude. You see, my father, Crystal's grandfather, owns the U-Pick-M Raspberry Farm next door – "

Crystal elbows her mom. "He knows all that, Mom."

Mrs. Nellson looks surprised. "Oh? I didn't know you two are friends."

"You don't know *everything* about me," she mutters under her breath.

"Crystaline," warns her dad, "don't talk to your mother like that…"

She rolls her eyes and crosses her arms while I step back and wish for instant invisibility. After an awkward pause where Crystal and her dad wage a silent glaring war, Mrs. Nellson continues.

"Anyway, Roland, this whole problem with your little beagle getting loose in his raspberries last summer was the funniest thing that's happened to our family in a very long time."

"Funny? So you're not mad?"

"Of course not. Well, I should say that *we're* not mad, but my father is still fuming."

"I didn't let my dog go on purpose. Just like tonight, he escaped out the window."

"And we're glad he did. It's a bit complicated, but during the last couple years, my father's been suffering from periodic depression. His health has been bad, and he's been thinking about giving up his farm and selling out to the developers. The trouble with your little beagle was just the thing to get him energized again."

Crystal giggles. "Yeah, every time he works with the new plants he grumbles about how *he's* not letting a mutt destroy *his* life."

"And I think he enjoyed reconnecting with your grandma, too," adds Mrs. Nellson, her eyes twinkling again.

"She says she used to know him pretty well when they went to high school together. That was before he left Snowville to go fight in World War II?"

"Grandpa has the hots for Roland's grandma?" interrupts Crystal, pretending to gag. "That's a match made in heaven…"

"More likely somewhere else," grumbles her dad.

Mrs. Nellson gives them both an irritated look before turning back to me. "Please understand, Roland. I wasn't laughing about your mom's accident. It was just so funny to find out that my father has gotten himself in a dither about your frisky little dog again."

"Did Grandpa call the police?" asks Crystal, looking worried.

"Of course. The ambulance, too."

"That means the whole Snowville Rescue Squad is on its way," says Mr. Nellson. "I'd better let them know it's a false alarm. The last thing we need right now are more problems with the authorities."

Crystal's dad sidles in around Mrs. Nellson as she gives me a puzzled look. "If your mom doesn't need help, Roland, to what, then, do we owe the pleasure of your visit?"

"Oh, um – I came to get my notebook." I wiggle my eyebrows and give Crystal what I hope is a look full of secret meaning.

"What note – Oh, I get it!" she says.

Mrs. Nellson narrows her eyes thoughtfully. "Hmm, I think I'll go in and stop my father from alerting the National Guard. You two can figure out the notebook situation yourselves. But remember, Crystaline, don't talk long. It's a school night."

As soon as she disappears down the hall, I gesture for Crystal to step outside. "Listen! I came to warn you! A white pickup truck was waiting in the parking lot at school. It followed you home and the driver was skinny and pale, just like you said."

"And you guys ran into him?"

"Yeah, it was horrible, but it was kind of his fault because he was parked by your driveway with his lights off. And he has a gun! Nose got out and started to bite his pants and then he threatened to shoot him. He might have gone after us, too!"

"Shhh, don't panic. Is he still out there?"

"No, he took off. And look!" I pull out the crumbly piece of veggie paddy and give it to Crystal. "A bunch of these dumped out of a cardboard box from his truck."

She holds it in the light. "Eeew, Roland. This is disgusting."

"It's from school, Crystal. Don't you see? He's transporting more stolen food!"

"I don't think so, Roland. This is already cooked. It's probably leftovers from lunch today. Or garbage."

"But why would he have it? And why was he following you?"

"How do I know? Look, someone's coming up the driveway."

"Quick! Get me a notebook." I turn to wave at Mom while Crystal goes in and passes out a pink spiral notebook with hearts and flowers doodled all over the front.

"That guy might come back tonight," I whisper to her through the screen door.

"I'll be all right. We have a motion detector security system. He won't get near the house without my dad knowing about it."

"That must be how your dad knew I was coming, too."

"Yep, and Roland? Don't worry about my grandpa. He deserves to be aggravated, 'coz he's such an animal hater. They give him trouble all the time. Deer, raccoons, chipmunks, *beagles*…"

"Okay, it's no biggy. I'm just glad I could warn you tonight."

"Good. Mission accomplished. See you tomorrow."

I wave good-bye as I slip down the steps and climb into our van.

"Did you get what you needed?" asks Mom as she inches away.

"Yeah, thanks. Did the police give you a ticket?"

"No, I was lucky. Little Bradley Copper was the officer. I used to baby-sit for his parents when I was in high school. He said he got a call about a big crash. He was relieved that it was just me stuck on the ice."

"Did he say who made the phone call?" I'm not going to mention the beagle-hating Alfred Rodriguez unless I have to. The idea of Grandma and him as a couple is way more than I can handle.

"No, but he said that if the other driver doesn't want to file a report and we don't even know who he is, then there's nothing we can do. He thinks that it would be wasteful to get our bumper repaired since our van probably won't last much longer anyway."

"I used to see his mother at Garden Club meetings, but she stopped coming a few years ago," adds Grandma. "Little Bradley Copper was always such a nice young man. Still is. Even Nose likes him."

"I hope Nose totally ignored him," I mutter.

"Oh, he did. He slept through the whole thing."

"Bradley said that it's a good idea to keep current about who my son is associating with. What *exactly* did he mean by that, Roland Wilbur Weedervich?" she asks, glaring at me through the rearview mirror.

"Are you hanging out with delinquents?"

Uh oh. Make parents think you're on their side, never lie to mothers, make the best use of what you have, never lie, make the best use...

The only things I have on hand are Dad's lame comeback lines. Are they lies? Will they work with Mom?

"Roland? Answer me right *now!* What was he..."

"Who cares? I mean, he says stuff like that all the time, especially in his antidrug classes. The guy needs to get a life. Whatsit to..."

Before I can finish, our van skids on another slick patch and totally distracts Mom away from her interrogation. And then the hills leading to Grandma's house on Western Reserve Avenue get even icier, so we're all completely silent. But I keep Dad's comeback line ready, just in case. I don't think I'll need it, though. Hopefully, Mom's nervousness will make her forget all about my delinquent associates – forever.

This is the first time since Nose joined our family that he doesn't perform his usual ritual of frantically tearing through the house in search of crumbs as soon as we get home. The only running he does tonight is straight

Chapter 15

to his bed under the utility room sink, where he curls up and immediately starts to snore.

I feel like crashing, too, but once again, diabetes stops me from doing what I *want* to do and instead, makes me do what I *have* to do. Before I can turn in, I need to eat something made out of carbohydrates in order to balance out my last insulin shot so I don't get hypoglycemia during the night. I go over and check out the new groceries that are still out on the kitchen counter. Bingo. There's fresh bakery bread.

"Shall I make you some toast, Grandma? Mom bought some of that sunflower oatmeal stuff you like."

"That'd be wonderful, honey. Can you bring it to my room?"

"I'll take some, too," calls Mom from the family room, where she's making a nest in her favorite reading chair. She sets a stack of library books on the table, drapes a fleecy Cleveland Browns blanket over her shoulders, and then pops a Mozart Piano Concerto into the CD player. When she leans back and folds her legs into the corner of the lumpy cushion, I suddenly remember all the times I used to crawl under that blanket with her. When I was a little kid, we had reading parties almost every night.

Then it hits me how much danger I put her in tonight. What if she'd been hurt in the accident? Or injured by that delivery guy? It'd be all my fault and she has no one to help her. No one but me. She looks startled when she glances over and sees me standing there, staring at her like some kind of zombie.

"What's wrong, Roland? Do you need something?"

I *can't* tell her that I want to get a book and climb in with her like I used to in the good old days. I *can't* say that I wish Dad was here to help, instead of only me all the time, that I'm lonely and scared, and everyone hates me, and most of all, I'm real sorry that I lied to her about the notebook tonight...

So instead of confessing all that mushy stuff, I cross my arms, tap my foot impatiently, and mumble, "Your long-suffering servant wishes to know how you'd like your toast, madame."

She groans and rubs her eyes. "Just plain, sir. And Roland? You'd better check your blood sugar after all the excitement tonight. You know how stress makes it go higher than usual."

"As you wish." I bow and back away into the kitchen, feeling a little better that there's something I can do to make up for all the trouble I've caused.

After I test my blood sugar, serve the toast, check to make sure that Grandma has actually eaten hers, and then eat a couple slices myself, I have just enough energy to turn on my computer and check my E-mail. There's two new messages. I open Dad's first.

To: rw@dirtnet.utt.net
From: prof_latweed@uninet.scifi.com
Date: Nov. 29, 7:59 P.M.

Hi, son. I suddenly got the strongest urge to talk to you. Are you in trouble? Did you use any of those lethal comeback lines today? E-mail me before you go to bed tonight so I know that you're OK. My flight to Iceland leaves first thing tomorrow morning, so I'll call you on Saturday, or else when I get home. Love you. Dad.

I press the reply button, type 'I'm fine', send it, and then open the second message. It's from Warthog and consists of only one line.

To: rw@dirtnet.utt.net
From: thehog@IOL.edu
Date: Nov. 29, 8:17 P.M.

meet me 4 a private at 9:30, your time

I check my watch. It's 9:27. Nothing like being just in time. I delete Warthog's E-mail message, close the mail file, and open the communication center where we always meet. I select our regular computer tech chatroom and scroll down the list of screen names of everyone who's currently logged on. He's already there. I type in a greeting, and we both exit out for a private conversation.

Rol: I thought u were grounded.

Hog: Nah. I'm home alone for another hour. Did U tell those granny leg wimps at your school where to get off?

Rol: Didn't have time. 2 busy.

Hog: That's bogus. U R never busy.

Rol: How's this for the last 3 hours? I had a date with an older babe who was stalked by an armed mobster. She dragged me into the girls locker room and later a cop grabbed me and nearly busted us 4 trespassing. And then my demented mother rammed into the mobster with our van, so I had to go to the older babe's house and warn her that he's coming after her.

Hog: U R so full of...

Rol: All true.

Hog: Yeah, right, and I'm an NBA All-Star who's just signed a trillion buck contract. What's this so-called babe's screen name? I'd know her if she's worth anything.

Rol: She's not wired.

Hog: She's never online?

Rol: Never.

Hog: Whoa, that's sick, dude. Dump her.

Rol: Can't. She needs my help.

Hog: Have U totally 4gotten where U parked your brain?

Rol: No. I'm straight like always. I've got to find the armed mobster.

Hog: Post a notice on all the boards.

Rol: This guy's not into electronics. He's a camouflage warrior type. Your basic Neanderthal.

Hog: Who cares about this creep anyway? Are U some kind of KISA?

Rol: Maybe. Define KISA.

Hog: KNIGHT IN SHINING ARMOR.

Rol: Yeah, that's me, and if the older babe doesn't find out who the mobster is, her mom might go to jail for something he did.

Hog: Maybe he's not as bad as U think. Like the granny leg thing. That was bogus, right? Maybe the babe's old lady's the real creep and she's trying to blame everything on the guy.

Rol: So u think that the nice mom lady is a crazed mobster and the crazed mobster is a nice mom lady?

Hog: Yeah, something like that, 'coz things ain't always what they seem, dude. Creeps ain't always creeps.

Rol: But older hot babes are always older hot babes.

Hog: Only if they're wired.

Rol: u r so lame.

Hog: At least I don't make up stories about girls locker rooms.

Rol: I was there.

Hog: Yeah? How many showers were there?

Rol: Who has time to count?

Hog: How many panties did U collect?

Rol: That's not my thing.

Hog: So what's the proof?

Rol: A witness.

Hog: Who? Older hot babe?

Rol: The one and only.

Hog: You're doomed, dude. Gotta go. E me when U have some REAL news.

We both exit the chatroom and he vanishes from the screen. I'm guessing his parents came home early. Ordinarily I'd hang out in cyberspace until ten o'clock, but tonight I shut down early. My eyes are too tired to read anymore, plus I can't stop thinking about what Warthog said. He's right about things not always being what you think

90

they are.

What if Crystal's mom *is* guilty? The Nellsons seem okay, but they could be a bunch of criminals, for all I know. Didn't Crystal say they're having a tough time with that competing stable opening up? Their money troubles could be getting desperate, and it just makes sense that desperate people do desperate things. Maybe that's the *real* reason Mr. Nellson didn't want the authorities showing up tonight. And what did the delivery guy say when he gave Crystal the food?

Your mom will know what to do with it.

Could Officer Copper be right? Could that guy really be Mrs. Nellson's accomplice? Was he bringing her more stolen food tonight? What if Mrs. Nellson actually *gave* Crystal her keys so she could destroy evidence tonight?

The Nellson Gang might be trying to play me for a sucker so that I'll end up getting all the blame. Why else would Crystal be so eager for me to snoop into the computer records? And look how easily she lied to Officer Copper! She was so smooth with that glove fight story that she must have lots of practice making stuff up. She staged a big act for Officer Copper, so maybe she was only *pretending* to be upset in the library this morning, too.

I try to go to sleep, but all these doubts keep me tossing and turning until I finally realize that I can't do anything about it tonight, no matter what great idea suddenly pops into my head. I'll just have to straighten it all out when I see Crystal again in the morning. Thinking of those magical green eyes of hers reminds me that almost anything can happen when she's around. Like the miracle of how I morphed from Fog Man into KISA in just one day. If she can do that, she can do anything.

Maybe even save her mom.

Chapter 16

How could I be such a moron? I've been sticking needles into myself for nine months – 260 days in a row – and now, the first time that I actually *want* to go to school, I lose my mind and forget to do the two things that I absolutely *have* to do every single morning for the rest of my life.

Test and inject. Test and inject. Test and inject.

Forever.

And I didn't do either one.

Stupid, cursed diabetes! I hate it! I hate everything about it!

Sitting in my usual front seat on the bus, I fume silently to myself as I pat the small pocket on the outside of my book bag. Great! My spare insulin kit is gone! Officer Copper put it back last night, but did he zip it shut? It might have slipped out as Crystal and I were rushing away. My only hope is that someone put it in the lost-and-found box in the Regurge-a-Dirge Factory. But if it's not there, wouldn't it be okay – just this once – to pretend to be normal for a day?

I might be able to pull it off… all I had for breakfast were two hard-boiled eggs, which are mostly protein and fat – hardly any carbohydrates – so if I skip lunch and my regular snacks, then maybe there won't even be enough sugar in my blood to need the missed insulin. It'd be like fasting.

Dr. Greystone and Mom would never find out.

No one would.

Wait a minute! Mr. Copper is right! My brain *must* be a couple doughnuts short of a dozen! Grandma always cuts corners like this and has nothing but trouble. I can't end up like her! No – I *won't* end up like her! Not now. Not ever. So there's no getting around it. If my insulin kit doesn't show up at school, I *have* to go back home. But it's going to be so lame. I'll miss study hall, so I won't be able to meet Crystal and then she'll panic and start recruiting fifty other guys before I can even…

"Hey, Wee Wee Weird-er-vich!" shouts someone behind me.

"Shields up! Incoming!"

I see something flying toward me out of the corner of my eye, but I duck down too late. Splat! A soft gooey thing smacks into the top of my head. A group in the back of the bus makes missile sounds and bursts out laughing as delicious smells explode around me. I'd know them anywhere. Double chocolate cake. Creamy marshmallow filling. Thick fudge frosting. Like poison to me without my morning insulin shot, but right up there with my all-time favorite foods.

"Yooze kids gotta stop all dat noise, r-r-right now!" warns Moonman, glaring red-eyed into the rearview mirror. But the laughing and scuffling gets wilder as a green apple ricochets off my shoe and drops slowly down the steps, thump, thump, thump, until it finally settles in a corner by the bus door.

"It's detention for dah apple thrower!" he shouts as he opens the door a couple inches to let it out onto the street.

"Moony, Moony, sauerkraut, Moony is a loony lout," they chant softly, their faces hidden so he can't see who's doing it.

Meanwhile, most of the cake bomb has fallen inside my jacket, so I scoot forward a couple inches to let it drop out onto the seat behind me, then snake my hand back to mold it into a hard little ball. I wait until Moonman stops at school to unload, and without turning around, I catapult it backwards over my shoulder.

"Ugh!" someone grunts. It's perfect timing. I bail out of the bus and escape to the Regurge-A-Dirge Factory while everyone else retreats to their lockers. Successful retaliation makes up for chocolate-smeared hair, but not for the empty lost-and-found box in the office. And to make things even worse, Mrs. Allsaggy, Snowville's only truly evil resident, is in charge of the office this morning. I have to stand at the counter forever, cracking my knuckles and clearing my throat, before her stork-like nose finally catches a whiff of my hair.

"Yes?" she chirps, visibly disappointed to see me instead of the giant chocolate marshmallow she was hoping for.

"Excuse me, ma'am. May I please use the telephone? I have to call home." Even at times like this, I can't turn the politeness off.

"You know the rules," she squawks. "No kids allowed. Use the pay phone next to the gym." She adjusts her bifocals, fluffs up her feathery orange hair, and ignores me again as she looks down to claw through the papers on her desk.

I rap on the counter twice before her flaring nostrils shoot up again. "Sorry, but I *can't* use the pay phone. I don't have any money."

"Is this an emergency?" she sniffs.

"Yes, it's an emergency." I sniff too, copying her tone exactly.

"What's so important that it can't wait until you get home?"

"It's private."

That sounds better than quoting the confidentiality rules – word for complicated word – that are supposed to protect my medical privacy in Section 504 of the Rehabilitation Act of 1973 *and* the Americans with Disabilities Act of 1990, which I could do… But by the look on her face, getting back to her stack of paperwork is all she really cares about.

"Did you forget your homework, because you know as well as I do that forgotten homework is not considered an emergency here at Snowville Middle School. Students your age should be…"

"No, ma'am. It's not about homework."

"What's the matter, then?" With her scrawny, blue-veined neck extended, her X-ray eyes attempt to probe my jacket pockets.

"I forgot to do something – *important*…"

She huffs, squints at me over her narrow bifocals, and then frowns at the clock. "You're the Weedervich boy, aren't you? Don't we have a Medical Management Plan on file for you?"

I nod, bracing for the inevitable diabetes questions. But Mrs. Allsaggy isn't a member of my school health team – she's affiliated with Grandma, instead.

"Your grandmother is in my gardening club, so I'll make an exception *this* time. Use that phone – " She's interrupted by the tardy bell. "Congratulations," she crows. "You're tardy *and* unexcused."

I turn away from her while I call home, hoping that my fudgy hair will give her an irresistible urge to rush out to the candy machine and leave me alone for awhile. The phone rings six times before Mom finally answers.

"I'm dripping from the shower, Roland. I can't come right now."

"That's okay. Take your time. I only had eggs for breakfast. Nothing sugary. No toast."

"How could you be so careless?"

"We all got up late. I just forgot, that's all. And anyway, I didn't even have to tell you. I could have just skipped it and you would have never known the difference."

"No, calling me is the right thing to do, but why don't you just use your spare insulin?"

"I don't have it. I think it fell out in the van last night."

"That's exactly why I always ask you about it, son. I'll look for it and if I can't find it, I'll bring your regular supplies for you to use there at school. It's silly for you to miss class by coming all the way home."

I whisper thanks and hang up, hoping that it takes her at least an hour to dry her hair and get dressed. That way, I won't miss seeing Crystal. I'm already a few minutes late to study hall and by the time I finish labeling South America's major land forms and sign out for the library, she's already there, waiting for me in the back storeroom. Her hair is long and loose today with a green ribbony thing clipped above one ear. It matches her sweater, which matches her eyes. Very cute. She looks tired, though. And grouchy.

"It's about time you showed up. I was beginning to think you weren't coming. I need that notebook I gave you last night." I nod and dig it out of my book bag as she continues, "And I can't wait to tell you what my mom said after you left."

"That's okay. I don't think I can stand anymore lousy news."

"It's not bad. She likes you. She said you're a nice young man."

"That's exactly what my grandma said about Officer Copper. He's the one who responded to your grandpa's 911 call."

"Oh, no. Did he tell on us?"

"Not really." I decide not to mention his warning about who I'm associating with, just in case he's right about the Nellsons.

"It's a good thing you were wearing your diabetes tag last night. I thought he was going to arrest you for having that syringe. Do you always have it with you?"

"Yeah, but I lost it last night. Do you have it?"

She shakes her head. "I didn't know that you're diabetic."

"Yes, you did. My grandma mentioned it at the mall."

"Really? I don't remember. I mean, mostly we were all so busy looking at her leg that we hardly listened to what she was saying."

"Your mom's on my school health team. She never told you?"

"Nope. Why would she?"

"I guess she wouldn't. I mean, it's no one's business but mine."

"And anyway, I didn't really know you until yesterday. Wouldn't it have been great if it snowed so much last night that school was cancelled today? I hardly slept at all, worrying about that weirdo following me home."

"Yeah, too bad they got all the roads cleared off. Have you had any new ideas about how to find that guy?"

"Well, maybe..." She looks puzzled and leans toward me. "Do you smell chocolate?"

"I ride on Moonman's bus –"

"Oh! I heard about a food fight," she giggles. "You got nailed with the cake?"

I nod and show her the top of my head. "Crystal, that delivery guy saw our license plate, so he might find us before we find him. Is there another reason for him to be at school last night besides stalking you? Maybe he's not really as bad as we think he is."

"He might play basketball."

"Not in boots and camouflage hunting clothes. And the game was still going on when he left to follow you."

"Do you think he was at school to meet with someone?"

"Maybe. Who was here last night?"

She twists a strand of hair as she tries to remember. "Let's see. Little Bradley Copper was here of course, and the basketball players. We heard someone vacuuming and we smelled old Mr. Fumesclinker burning something, but we don't know for sure if he was here since we didn't actually see him."

"It's a good thing, too," I grumble. "I see *way* too much of him already. His pants were *miles* south of the equator this morning, if you know what I mean."

"Eeew, Roland. You're making me sick."

"How do you think I feel every morning?"

"You don't have to look at him."

"I always sit in the front seat."

"But you don't *have* to sit in front. I mean, just 'coz it's a habit, you can change. Why torture yourself?"

Before I can answer, the bell rings and we get up to leave. "Hold on," says Crystal, "I forgot to give you these printouts. I think they're from the lunchroom."

She pulls a wad of computer paper out of her purse. "Maybe you could look at 'em today, but I need 'em back before you go home. I stole 'em from my mom's desk so I have to put 'em back before she finds out." She slips them into my three-ring binder and gives me a secret little wave before taking off down the hall.

"Wait! Where shall I meet you?"

"For what?" she says, walking backwards.

"You know, to give these back to you?" I hold up the printouts.

"Meet me in front of the girls locker room. Right after school."

This must be some kind of world's record! The girls locker room – two days in a row! I hurry to my next class, Computer Lab, and sit down just as Mr. Macintosh starts to give instructions for a test on the history of computer programming. I aced the pretest, so instead of having to take it again, I'll have some free time to study Crystal's printouts.

The first page is a memo dated November third to Mrs. Nellson. It requests an explanation for October's inventory discrepancies. This might be more complicated than I thought. What's an inventory discrepancy?

The next page has six columns. Item. Unit cost. Vendor. Amount checked in. Amount checked out. Amount on hand. In the first column, there's a long list of foods. The next column is how much they cost, and a vendor sells stuff, so the third column identifies the companies that the school buys food from. Some lines are highlighted in pink, probably the missing foods.

item	unit cost	vendor	# check in	# check out	# on hand
cabbage	$1/head	VEG-ALL	25	12	13
pea soup	$.69/can	VEG-ALL	38	16	22
sugar	$.50/lb	SWEET-T	50	35	15

If the highlighted items are all from the same company, this could be the evidence that gets Mrs. Nellson her job back. Then all we'd have to do is figure out how the delivery guy fits in. I scan the pink lines, page after page, and then go back to check them a little slower. According to this, the stolen food came from a bunch of different places, not just one or two, so it's not likely that they'd *all* be cheaters. That means our idea about a company overbilling the school is probably wrong and Crystal's mom, or someone else connected with the lunchroom, looks more guilty than ever.

And then it hits me that Mrs. Nellson has known about the missing food for almost a month. Today is November 30. She's had this printout for 27 days, so she's also had 27 days to concoct a story and cover her tracks. I flip over to the next section, September's record, and find only two highlighted lines. The last section, August, has no missing food, which makes sense since we didn't even start school until the end of the month. So according to this, most of the food disappeared in October. I search through again, looking for a record of November…

"Roland Weedervich? Are you awake? Didn't you hear the intercom announcement?"

I close the printouts and cover them with my elbow while Mr. Macintosh marches toward me. "No, sir. What announcement?" I ask, trying to ignore the snickering kids looking up from their tests.

"Mrs. Allsaggy needs you in the office. She said your grandmother is here with your diabetes medication?"

His stern face softens with pity before he turns away to address the class. "Back to work, sixth-graders. You have just ten more minutes to finish."

When they settle down, he leans over and whispers, "I didn't know that you're a diabetic. I thought the administration was supposed to inform us about students with serious medical issues. What if you went into shock in my class? I would have never guessed. After all, you don't look like one."

"Look like one? What does that mean?" I'm suddenly shaking so hard, I'm afraid I might puke in his face.

"You know, unhealthy pasty skin with big pores and lots of sweat. And overweight? Aren't you too skinny to be diabetic?"

My throat gets so tight I couldn't say anything even if I wanted to, so I shove Crystal's printouts into my book bag and push out my chair.

"You're the best computer student I've ever had, Roland, and I'm real sorry to hear about this. Believe me, I know *all* about it because my uncle was blinded by diabetes. He's dead now, but I used to help him when I was your age. Take all the time you need in the office this morning. And don't hesitate to come to me if you ever need help. My door is always open."

I nod, gather up my stuff, and with blurry eyes, run from the Computer Lab. Too angry and embarrassed to watch where I'm going, I slam into the first set of lockers so hard, one of the doors pops open and hits me in the shoulder. Then someone's art project, an ugly, unfinished mask, crashes down and just misses my chocolate-smeared head.

That's it! I've had enough! I flatten the bizarre smirk of the mask with a single stomp of my size-ten sneakers and continue on toward the office, wiping away what I hope is my final tear.

I'm so mad, I can't even figure out who to take it out on. That witchy Mrs. Allsaggy for announcing my diabetes over the intercom, all the lamebrain idiots who heard it, big-mouthed Grandma for blabbing in the office, the cake-throwing slobs on the bus, snoopy Mr. Macintosh for being so sappy. And stupid. What does his fat, blind uncle have to do with me, anyway? He knows one dead guy with diabetes and thinks he's an expert. He can keep his door locked from now on, for all I care!

The worst part is, the deep down *smart* part of me clearly knows who's *really* to blame. *I'm* the one who's blowing everything up into such a big deal. But the thin-skinned touchy guy who's having a tantrum right now is too overwhelmed to admit it. And even though I tell myself a million, zillion times to get a grip and chill out, I still can't shake the sick feeling that the really bad stuff hasn't even happened yet.

Grandma always says, when it rains, it pours. And the way things are going so far today, I know I'm in for a real soaker.

Grandma's electronic hat is flashing purple lights and buzzing, "Lavender blue, dilly, dilly…" when I storm into the Regurge-a-Dirge Factory. She's leaning over the counter in a cozy head-to-hat huddle with Mrs. Allsaggy and neither

Chapter 17

of them looks up until I throw down my book bag.

"Is this my stuff?" I mutter, pointing at a lacy crocheted bag that's dangling from the black handle of Grandma's three-legged cane.

"Yes, dear, and it's lovely to see you, too," says Grandma with a sly wink at Mrs. Allsaggy.

I'd rather die than haul this frilly thing into the boys' bathroom, so I unhook its straps and dump my insulin supplies into my book bag before turning to leave, all in about five seconds. But Mrs. Allsaggy stops me before I can even open the door.

"Mr. Weedervich," she warbles, "where do you think you're going?" It's amazing how sweet her voice is in front of Grandma.

I stop and glare at her, too upset to answer. Grandma must realize that I'm about to lose it, because she jumps in to try to help. "Oh, let him go, Doris. He'll be right back. This little procedure just takes a minute or two."

"I'm sorry, Sophie, but students are not allowed to possess drugs at school. The school nurse will have to accompany him."

"Into the bathroom?" I ask.

"If necessary," she sniffs, her spiked nose rising.

"But I don't have any drugs. This is medication from my doctor."

Grandma looks shocked that I'd argue like that, but after the morning I've had, I think I'm being pretty polite.

Mrs. Allsaggy stretches her thin lips into a fake smile and says, "We want what's best for you, sweetie, so take those drugs to the nurse's office. As you know, the dispensary is the second door on the right." She flicks a chipped orange fingernail toward the short hallway leading to the inner chambers of the Regurge-a-Dirge Factory.

I scowl at Grandma. "Why didn't you sign me out? That way I could leave and do this in the van without any hassle at all."

"I'm sorry, Roland. I didn't know. Next time…"

"There won't be a next time," I hiss.

"Come this way," sings Mrs. Allsaggy.

I take a deep breath and trudge down the hallway to the nurse's office. The door's closed, so I tap lightly, but no one answers. I tap a little louder and glance back over my shoulder. Both Grandma and Mrs. Allsaggy are watching me like a couple of beady-eyed vultures, so I try the doorknob and just let myself in.

I sit down and line up my supplies on the nurse's desk. In just a few seconds, I insert a fresh lancet into my finger-pricker, pull the trigger, squeeze a full drop of blood out onto a new test strip, and slip it into my electronic meter. So far so good. While I'm waiting for a reading, I notice a big cardboard box overflowing with shredded paper and empty cartons. It's labeled, READY FOR BURNING. Moonman must not have gone around collecting yet today.

When my meter beeps, I'm not surprised that the amount of sugar in my blood is much higher than usual. I don't want the nurse to walk in on me, so I get right to work and draw slightly more insulin than usual into a syringe, pull up my shirt, bunch up some skin on my stomach, and stick in the needle. Ouch! The insulin is cold after being outside, so it stings as it first goes in. I make sure everything's sealed and toss my supplies back in my book bag so I can smuggle them past Mrs. Allsaggy, just in case I need them again today. She's yakking on the phone when I get back to Grandma, so it's easy to slip by.

"Where's Mom?" I say as softly as I can.

"Outside in the van. A truck was blocking the handicapped space, so she's waiting in a no parking zone and has to be ready to move if a traffic officer comes along. There weren't any other spaces."

"I'll walk out with you," I say, holding the office door for her as she grasps the handle of her cane with one hand and her bizarre pink and green purse with the other.

"How was your sugar?" she asks, her voice too loud as usual.

"Shhh, Grandma. We have to be quiet in the hall." The smell of baking pizza hits us full blast as I lead her toward the bus ramp exit next to the lunchroom.

"Your number was high, wasn't it, Roland?"

"Yeah. It's a good thing you came."

"I knew it!" she shouts. "You've been sneaking treats, haven't you? You can't fool an old pro like me."

She stops to smell my hair. "Fudge marshmallow and pepperoni pizza. I can't imagine why you'd ruin them by mixing them together."

I laugh. "I'm not like you, Grandma. I wasn't eating any of it. Someone threw cake at me on the bus this morning and the pizza's coming from the lunchroom, not me."

She smiles. "That's an excuse I've never tried before. Do you think it'll work with your mother?"

I chuckle. "The truth always works with her."

She stops and gives me her pink and green monstrosity. "Take out a granola bar, dear, so you don't get low before lunch."

"Yeah, good idea." I check the halls, dig out the granola bar, unwrap it, stuff it in my mouth, and give her a quick hug before anyone shows up. "Thanks for bailing me out this morning. I hope it wasn't too much trouble."

"Not at all, honey. Your mother and I are glad you called," she yells, leaning against me. "That's what family's for. We always help each other, no matter what."

That reminds me of Crystal and her family. Helping is what she's trying to do, too, but after looking at the printouts, I'm afraid that even her best efforts won't do much good.

I step outside and hold the door wide open for Grandma and her huge purple hat. It fills the whole doorway as she slips her purse onto the handle of her cane and stops to search her pockets for matching purple gloves. Our mini van is parked illegally in the fire lane next to the bus ramp. The dents from the accident last night look almost as bad as the rust around the doors, but Mom doesn't seem to mind. She's just sitting there relaxing, reading her *Snowville Drifter,* and drinking hot tea. She glances up, then rolls down her window.

"Roland? Can you go back to Mr. Dirge's office and get me a copy of the December parent volunteer schedule? Nose ate mine before – "

Nose hears his name and leaps up to put his front paws on the dashboard, wagging and howling his usual greeting.

"Hi, boy!" I shout from the doorway.

He must think I'm calling him because he springs across and pounces through Mom's *Drifter,* ripping it neatly in half. But even worse, his tail hammers her arm and spills hot tea all over her legs.

"Ouch! Go on! Get off!"

For once in his life, Nose obeys. He gets off of her, and quickly, too, right through his favorite opening, the van window. He races up the ramp toward me, but I can't shut the door because Grandma's still standing in it, so I keep holding it open with one hand, throw down my book bag with the other, and get ready to grab him as soon as he gets close. But when he smells the pizza behind us, he forgets all about me. He swerves away and darts between Grandma's legs, his white-tipped tail disappearing under her skirt and into Snowville Middle School.

"Grandma! Watch out! I have to go back inside!"

She looks confused and moves over just enough for me to squeeze in around her hat. When Nose's excited howl echoes through the open door, she steps back inside, too.

"Oh, no! Roland! Stop that little beast!"

"Don't worry. I'll get him!"

But just when I'm about to lure him away from the lunchroom door, the class-changing bell ruins everything! It suddenly goes off, making him panic and take off like a misfired rocket, zigzagging wildly from wall to wall as dozens of doors swish open, releasing hundreds of pent-up middle school kids, all at the same time.

You'd think he's a skunk instead of a beagle for all the hysteria that breaks out. The last I see of him, his wagging tail is swallowed by a mob of rioting girls, half of them squealing, "Oooh! A cute little puppy!" while the other half screams, "Help! A smelly yucky hound!"

How could a silent hallway morph into complete pandemonium so fast? The girls' screeching and Nose's howling are noisy enough, but when you add Mrs. Allsaggy's booming intercom appeals for calm, sirens approaching from City Hall, and all the first floor teachers' thunderous demands for immediate order, you have everything needed to create the loudest place on earth.

Poor Nose has no idea what he's gotten himself into, so he does the only thing he's good at. He tries to escape by running around in even bigger circles, much faster than before. There's such an uproar, I can't separate his high-pitched howl from the rest of the noise. I can guess where he's headed, though, by the way the crowd moves, dipping and weaving, doubling back, then spinning around in frenzied chaos. From where Grandma and I are watching by the bus ramp exit, it looks like a Chinese dragon has busted loose in the middle of the hallway.

I don't tell Grandma this, but after the morning I've had, the touchy, thin-skinned part of me is glad Nose is stirring up so much trouble. I hope he leads his rowdy followers straight across Mrs. Allsaggy's desk, and through the Computer Lab, too. And the best thing about this whole mess is that no one suspects who Nose belongs to. At least, not yet.

"Roland! What are we going to do?" Grandma's head is wobbly like it was yesterday after school. And with her poor eyesight, there's no telling how much she's really understanding.

"We can't do anything, Grandma, until the next bell rings and everyone goes back to class. Do you have another granola bar?"

"No. Should I get some beagle bait from the kitchen?"

"Great idea. Let me help you so you don't get trampled."

I take Grandma's elbow and guide her through a side door that leads directly into the kitchen. As it closes behind her, I hear her calling, "Yoo hoo! Is anybody here?"

Back in the hallway, I spot a familiar green ribbon bobbing in the crowd. As if she feels me looking at her, Crystal turns around and waves.

She forces her way out and skips up to me, as infected with beagle mania as everyone else.

"That's your dog, isn't it?" she giggles. "I've got his voice memorized! I wish my grandpa was here! As soon as I heard – "

And then her sparkling eyes suddenly widen with horror as they focus on someone walking up the bus ramp and entering the building behind me. She throws her arms in the air and screams.

"Roland! Watch out! Murderer! Thief! Run for your life!"

She turns and sprints down the stairs leading to the school basement, wailing all the way. I look behind me to see what's wrong. *Yikes!* It's the delivery guy, coming my way. No! Not *my* way. He ignores me and rushes by with a fast, long-legged stride, straight downstairs! He's wearing camouflage clothes again and carrying a big burlap sack. And he's following Crystal!

Thank goodness Grandma comes right back. One of the cooks holds the door for her as she hobbles out with a plate of steaming hot pizza in one hand and her cane and purse in the other.

"Grandma! As soon as the next bell rings, you have to call Nose! Ask him if he's hungry, real loud. He always comes for food."

I start to leave, but then Grandma's cane suddenly gives me an idea for how to help Crystal.

"Stand here and wait for me, Grandma. I'll get you a chair."

I run into the lunchroom, pull a chair off the first table, and drag it into the hallway in full view of the rioting kids. As gently as I can, I make Grandma sit down and then grab her three-legged cane, swinging it like a baseball bat. It's too light to hit a home run, so I hoist it over my head and bring it down like a caveman's club. It's hollow aluminum is still too flimsy for what I have in mind. I start to panic. I need a weapon! *Now!*

Emergency Rule #1 runs through my head. *Make the best use of what you have. Make the best use, make the best use –* I look around. My book bag is still out on the bus ramp, but what about Grandma's purse? No, it's too small, and even putrid green and shocking pink isn't lethal enough to stop that creep. That leaves me with only one option. Iris!

She's solid. Strong. Kind of heavy. And Grandma's shoe is stiff and pointed. I'll probably be grounded for the rest of my life, but what else can I do?

I set Grandma's cane next to her chair and kneel down to shout into her ear, "Please, Grandma, I need to borrow your leg. I don't have time to explain, but please! Take it off! Fast!"

She looks at me like I've lost my mind. With all the commotion around us, I can see that I'm not getting through to her, and all I can think is that if I waste another second, I'll be too late to help Crystal.

It's totally gross, but I grit my teeth, lift Grandma's skirt away from her knee, loosen the connecting buckles, and just like that, Iris falls to the floor.

"Roland! What are you doing?"

"Grandma! I'm sorry! I have to go!"

I grab Iris and start for the basement. But before I go down, I turn around and shout, "Remember! Ask Nose if he's hungry. Then you have to grab his collar. I'll bring Iris right back, I promise. Just get Nose!"

I take off down the cement stairs into the basement, but as soon as I get to the bottom, I can see that I'm already too late. Crystal's not screaming anymore, the delivery guy is gone, and all I can hear is the deafening roar of Moonman Fumesclinker's trash-burning furnace.

Chapter 18

I stop at the bottom of the stairs and turn Iris upside down so the spiked toe of Grandma's shoe is on top like an ax. Her purple knee-high sock is slippery, so I get a better grip by pushing it toward the ankle. Okay. Now I'm armed and ready for anything. I take a few trial chops and adjust one hand for better balance.

Now what? I look around.

There're no footprints, no Crystal, and no demented delivery guy. The cinder block walls of the school basement are painted pale yellow, except where pipes and wires intersect and branch out into sturdy metal boxes and padlocked cabinets. A narrow fluorescent light hangs down between wide vents and casts deep shadows into all the cobwebbed corners. The dim light seems to aim straight down, as though it's being sucked into the rusty metal grates that are cut into the cracked concrete floor. Dust and soot cover everything, even a lopsided tower of plastic buckets and an overfilled barrel of crushed aluminum cans. I can't hear anything except the roar of loud mechanical whirling and grinding.

Think! If I was Crystal, where would I go?

My heart skips a beat as I realize that she must be hiding behind one of the four doors to my right. A sharp chemical odor seeps through the first one next to the stairs. This must be the dreaded Sanctum of Sanitation, a stinky black hole masquerading as a janitor's closet that swallows up the school's grungiest things, including a few middle school kids. Was Crystal desperate enough to go in there? The door is slightly open, but it's dark and I can't see anything inside. It's pretty obvious that the second door leads to the boiler room. It's painted red with a big warning sign. A heavy chain and thick padlock secure an iron bar across the third door. The only way Crystal can be in there is if someone threw her in and locked the door

EXTREME DANGER!
HIGH VOLTAGE AREA.
STAY OUT!!!!

from the outside, and I don't think there's been enough time for all that to happen. At least, I hope there hasn't.

A light shines through the bubbly glass window of the fourth door. I sneak toward it, walking on the sides of my shoes and cradling Grandma's leg next to my chest so I don't accidently knock over the tower of plastic buckets leaning up against the wall. I stop outside the door, stare at its brass doorknob, listen, and try my hardest to come up with a plan. Suddenly a phone starts to ring from inside. Once. Twice. *Yikes!* I practically drop Iris, my hands are so sweaty!

A man coughs a couple times, then answers the phone. "Hello? Yah? Dat's okay vit me. Yah? Okee-doe-kee. I'll be r-r-right dare."

It's Moonman!

He hangs up and says, "I can't help you now, Ed. Dat goofy Allsaggy voman vants me to catch a little doggy upstairs."

He's not alone! Could Crystal be in there, too?

"How long is that going to take?"

The second voice is hoarse and impatient, like the delivery guy!

"...because everything I got from you last night dumped out when this wacky lady and her crazy beagle rammed into my truck on my way home. I have to set the trap today, you know. I can't wait much longer with the weather turning cold like this."

Moonman chuckles. "Did you say cr-r-razy beagle? Dat's just vut dat Allsaggy voman said, too. Cr-r-razy beagle."

"Small world. So, how long will you be upstairs?"

"Who knows? Once dey got me, dey find so much for me to do."

"Should I help myself like I did last night?"

"Yah, may as vell. Dat food's in its usual place. I gotta get a r-r-rope from dat supply closet and den catch dat little doggy."

A chair scrapes and Moonman's silhouette appears through the glass. Oh, no! If he's headed for the janitor's closet, I have to hide! I already know that the next door is bolted shut, so my only hope is the boiler room. I dart over, twist the door knob, and pull the metal door open. Then I slip inside and jut my toe out just enough so that I can still see the office door through the crack.

Moonman comes out, pulls up his pants, tucks in his shirt, and limps by, as though one of his feet has gone to sleep. The furnace behind me is so loud I can't hear where he goes, but I assume he's getting rope from the supply closet next door. If Crystal's hiding in there, she'd better watch out!

I ease the door shut, rest Iris on my shoulder, take a deep breath, and pat the wall next to the door. Hopefully I'll find a light switch before I'm electrocuted. I feel one and flip it on. I guess I'm expecting something like the cramped and cluttered furnace room in Grandma's basement, because I'm shocked to see that Moonman's boiler room is as deep and wide as a warehouse. It spans the entire length of the whole school.

Old boxes and all types of garbage are heaped in a bin next to a big compacting machine that molds the trash into solid cubes that are stacked neatly along one wall. There's a huge furnace in back that's attached to some kind of rumbling fan with big vents running through it. Moonman must throw in a some garbage cubes every few minutes or so. Or hours. Who knows how long they last?

It's surprisingly free of smoke in here, but not smells. Geez, it stinks! Now I know why the school smelled so horrible last night. If Moonman was here and left the boiler room door open, this rotten garbage smell would have leaked straight upstairs into the main hallway. Does Crystal have enough willpower to hide in here without gagging?

"Crystal?"

I'm afraid to speak any louder than a whisper, but with the lights on, she must be able to see me if she's here. Unless she's buried under something and can't look out. Or already dead from the stinky fumes. I look a little closer at the trash bin and see that the top layer is dripping with scraps from yesterday's lunch. Then my toe nudges a box that's plastered with labels from Snowville Middle School Food Service. I pull open the top flap and discover giant cartons of strawberry gelatin mix, new and unopened. Is this part of Mrs. Nellson's missing inventory?

Has Moonman been stealing the school's food?

Just then the door opens behind me. Totally spooked, I jump and yell, and before I get a good look at who's coming in, I turn around and swing down with Iris as hard as I can. The pointed toe of Grandma's shoe lands with a sickening thud.

"Aaarggh!" And then the worst curses I've ever heard blast my way. Without even aiming, I've managed to chop the delivery guy dead center in the middle of his shoulder. His beady eyes look stunned at first, but then narrow with fury as they recognize me from last night.

"Why, you dirty little – " He steps toward me and tries to grab Grandma's leg. "Gimme that thing!"

I swing the leg to the left and pivot around toward the trash compactor. He stomps toward me, growling more curses, the skin of his bony face squished up with horrifying rage. He shoves me back against the trash cubes and starts to twirl his burlap sack over his head like a lasso. Then, like a striking snake, he whips it down at my head. I use Iris like a shield, but the sack wraps around Grandma's shoe just enough for him to try to pull it away.

I tighten my grip, spread my legs, and yank Grandma's leg as hard as I can. The sack loosens and I fly back into the compressed trash cubes just Crystal busts through the boiler room door, her long dark hair falling in a mess of curls around her face. She stops to catch her breath, fidgeting with the sleeves of her bright green sweater and anxiously chewing on her lower lip. Then her eyes adjust to the dim lighting and finally focus on the delivery guy.

"AHHH!" she screams, turning to run back out, but she freezes, her shoulder pressed against the open door, when he shouts, "Wait, little girl! Call the police! A maniac is attacking me!"

When she turns to look at me, I see that confusion has overtaken her fear. I sit up and use Iris to bat away some garbage. "No, Crystal! Run! Get help! He's trying to strangle me and he'll go after you next!"

He steps toward her just as Nose scampers down the stairs and starts running in frenzied circles outside the door, knocking over the tower of plastic buckets and tipping the barrel of crushed pop cans.

"Nose! Come here, boy!" I shout.

He darts toward Crystal, spots his old enemy from last night, and jumps up to latch onto his knee. Officer Copper and Moonman follow close behind, kicking buckets and cans out of the way.

"We're in the boiler room!" I holler.

Crystal leaps away from the door just as Brad Copper lumbers in, carrying a long pole with a leather loop dangling from one end. But he won't be needing it now. Nose has stopped rampaging and is licking the delivery guy's hand as fast as he can.

"Quick, Ed! Grab dat doggy's collar," shouts Moonman.

"No! Forget the dog," shouts Crystal, pointing at Ed. "That's the thief!"

"Who, me?" he says, baffled. "Officer, you're just in time! I've been assaulted by that violent delinquent over there in the trash! I think he's out of his mind on drugs."

"Me? On drugs?" I shout back. "It's not true! *He* attacked *me!* I was only defending myself."

Brad Copper glares at Crystal, Ed, and me, and then whacks his dog-catching pole against the cement floor like it's a giant conductor's baton.

"Everyone, be quiet!" he thunders.

We're all stunned into silence. Even Nose lets go of the Ed's leg and sits down, quietly tilting his head back and forth as he studies Officer Copper.

"What in the world is going on? One person at a time."

"I've been struck in the shoulder by…" Ed starts to say.

"No, he's the creep who's stalking me," interrupts Crystal, sidestepping over some garbage and offering me a hand out of the trash cubes.

"Yeah, she's right," I say, letting her pull me up. "I came down here to help her, but then he whipped me with his big sack."

"Yeah, and my mom is innocent," she adds.

And then we both shout together, "He's the thief!"

Our pointing gets Nose excited, so he throws his head back, belts out a good one, and clamps onto Ed's leg again.

"I said one at a time!" commands Officer Copper. "But before anyone says another word, give me that leg, Roland Weedervich. We don't want anyone else to get clubbed or batted or kicked or – whatever. Just hand the thing over."

"Okay," I say, surrendering Iris and brushing trash off my jeans, "but will you listen to what really happened? The first thing you should know is that Nose has nothing to do with any of this, so just pretend he isn't here."

"That's kind of hard to do, considering all the trouble he's caused this morning. You're forgetting that I already know what a destructive animal he is."

"He's just a puppy, Mr. Copper. Isn't it embarrassing for a huge guy like you to go after him with that big pole? I mean, look at him."

Nose seems to understand that he's the center of attention, because just then he lets go of Ed's leg and beelines happily toward me – and the garbage cubes. I pick him up and hold him tight before he can start digging into yesterday's lunch.

"What really matters, is that this is the guy who brought stolen food to Mrs. Nellson. He followed Crystal home from school last night, too, and then he came back today to steal more. He was planning to take it away in that big sack of his."

"Why, you lying, conniving, no-good little brat," Ed sputters as he steps toward me, fists clenched, stopping only when Brad Copper threatens him with Grandma's leg.

"No, R-R-Roland," says Moonman, stepping between us, "you got it all wrong. Dat's just trash and leftovers dat I burn in dis new furnace."

"This is trash?" I hold Nose tightly under one arm and show them the carton of strawberry gelatin I found earlier.

"Oh, no, dat shouldn't be here…"

"What a minute, Mr. Fumesclinker, one thing at a time." Brad

Copper turns toward Ed and says, "Who are you and what are you doing in this school building?"

Ed puffs out his ribs and looks indignant. "I'm Edward Stickwell, a law-abiding taxpayer and a US Veteran, and I resent being attacked and accused of crimes I have nothing to do with."

"Yah, he's my new neighbor. I asked him to come to school today. We're troubled by r-r-rabid r-r-raccoons all up and down our r-r-road. He vas bit a vile ago. Almost died from r-r-rabies."

"Please, Mr. Fumesclinker, I asked Mr. Stickwell, so if you could let him do the talking?"

"He's right, Officer. I have a permit to trap the raccoons. There's no way that I'm going to let anyone else in Snowville get bit and go through what I've just recovered from. I'm just here to pick up a few leftovers for my traps."

"What kind of leftovers?" asks Brad Copper.

"Trash from yesterday's lunch, I guess," he says, rubbing his sore shoulder and glaring at me again. "These kids are too spoiled and finicky to finish their plates."

"Are Roland and Crystal correct? Did you bring school food to the Nellson home last Wednesday afternoon?"

"Are you asking about the mock chicken legs I put in their freezer?" he says, scowling.

"And giant tuna," says Crystal.

"And ten pounds of sacked potatoes," I add.

Mr. Fumesclinker waves his hands with frustration. "No, no, no! Yooze are talking about dah tings I find in dah boxes. Dat vas dah first day Ed Stickwell vas here getting leftovers for his traps. I tell him to bring all dat stuff to Mrs. Nellson since he vas passing her house on his vay home. I had to stay here at dah school and I didn't vant the frozen stuff to go bad. I knew she'd know vut to do vit dem."

"Let me see if I understand," says Brad Copper, swinging Iris absentmindedly like a purple pendulum. "Mr. Fumesclinker, is it true that you collect trash to burn in this furnace?"

"Yah, it's true, but sometimes I got help dat's no good. Boys dat's got detention, dey do dah collecting." He turns to shake a fist at me. "Yooze got no sense, some of yooze kids, bringing me stuff dat's not even bad."

"Do you mean to say that students are responsible for gathering the trash? Even from the lunchroom?" presses Mr Copper.

"Especially dat lunchroom, vit tons and tons of food vasted every day. Dat's the best part of dis furnace. It burns dat stuff and turns it to heat. No more vaste."

"So last week some kids brought you those food items by mistake, thinking it was trash, when it was really good food?"

"I wouldn't go so far as to call it good…" I start to say.

"Would you mind not interrupting, Mr. Weedervich?" He turns back to Moonman and says sternly, "We believe that food was stolen."

"No, Ed's a good guy. He vas helping me by bringing it to Mrs. Nellson so she could take care of it."

"Why didn't you just put it in the school kitchen yourself?"

"No key. Dah lock vas changed and no one vas in der no more to let me in."

"Yes, that's true," agrees Brad Copper. "After items began showing up missing on the monthly inventory reports, we suggested that all the kitchen locks be changed. When more food was gone after that, we knew that the thief had to be someone with access, someone with the new set of keys."

"So that's why you thought it was my mom," says Crystal. "But how did you know where to look for the food at our house?"

"Another officer overheard some ladies talking about large food containers stored under your sink. It was just logical to check your freezer, too, since Mrs. Nellson was already a suspect because of the keys. It was precisely the kind of evidence we needed to solve the case."

Crystal and I nod to each other. She was right about her talkative Great Aunt Eunice.

"So, Mr. Fumesclinker," continues Mr. Copper, "don't you check all the boxes before burning them to make sure there's nothing of value inside?"

"Yah, dat's how I found dat bag of fake chicken, but other stuff just gets tossed r-r-right into dah compactor by dah detention boys. Some goes r-r-right into dah furnace, too. I never know. Principal Dirge supervises dem bad boys. I got lots of other tings to do."

Officer Copper keeps swinging Iris and nodding his head. "Well, that explains where the food has been going."

"Yeah, especially since it began disappearing in October when the weather got cold enough for Mr. Fumesclinker to start using that furnace," I add.

"How do you know about that?" asks Brad Copper suspiciously.

"Oh – um, just a lucky guess, sir."

"So, you're not stalking me? You were just doing a favor for Mr. Fumesclinker?" Crystal asks Ed Stickwell, her green eyes apologetic.

He nods, still rubbing his shoulder.

"And your missing teeth? Did they fall out when you had rabies?" she persists as she clears her hair away from her face and holds it up on top of her head in a loose pile of curls.

"I don't think that's any of our business, Miss Nellson," says Brad Copper, embarrassed.

"No, I don't mind, officer. People ask me all the time. I got hit in the mouth while I was stationed in Iraq during the first Gulf War in 1991. But I lost so much weight and got so dehydrated after that raccoon gave me rabies, my false teeth don't fit anymore. And they hurt like heck. I'm hoping my gums will go back to normal so I won't have to go into debt buying new ones."

He pauses to rub his mouth self-consciously, and then turns to point at bony finger at me. "Now it's *my* turn to ask a few questions. You with the wild beagle – what are you, some kind of prosthetic gladiator?"

I look down, my face turning red. "Sorry about clobbering you," I mumble. "I hope your shoulder isn't too sore. And I'll replace the pants Nose tore up last night, too."

"Nah, don't worry about it. They were already rags, but I can think of another way you can make it up to me... How about letting me borrow your dog sometime?"

"My dog? You want Nose to do something?" Everyone else looks as startled as I am. "I don't think he'd be much good for anything, sir. He's never hunted, except this one time when he went after rasp..."

Ed Stickwell rolls his eyes at the others and then interrupts with a grin, "You're right, he's no good for hunting. Actually, I was needing him for a much *harder* job, one that I can't keep up with even when my shoulder doesn't hurt like this... Do you suppose you could let your dog loose in my house once a week so I'll never have to use the vacuum cleaner again?"

Surprised, everyone laughs and then looks at me, so I look at Nose, who climbs up my neck and starts licking the chocolate spot on top of my head.

"Does that sound fun, little guy?" I say, struggling to keep him still.

He yips and tries to squirm away. "I think he's just agreed," I say, my face burning with embarrassment. "As long as there aren't any more rabid raccoons around your place, that is. And don't worry, Mr. Fumesclinker, I'll pick up all those cans and buckets that Nose scattered around out there by the stairs."

"Dat vill be okee-doe-kee, R-R-Roland."

I turn to Brad Copper next. "I'm almost afraid to ask, sir, but did Nose mess up anything upstairs, too?"

He smiles and shakes his head. "Not this time."

"Good. That leaves just one more problem, then. I never thought I'd have to say this again, but I should hurry upstairs to see how my grandma's doing, so Mr. Copper? Could you – well, I need that – um, I mean, would you *please pass Grandma's leg?*"

Everyone laughs again, even harder than before. And this time, so do I.

Chapter 19

My jump shots into the barrel are right on target this morning, so it only takes a couple minutes for Crystal and me to pick up the aluminum cans and restack the plastic buckets.

"You should be on the basketball team with that shot, Roland. Or is your aim only deadly with cans?"

"No, I'm pretty good with spitballs, too. I'm thinking about starting a Blizzard Basketcan team. No dribbling, and you get to drink the pop…"

Crystal giggles and reaches over to pet Nose as we start to climb the stairs together. "Thanks, Roland! You and Nose saved my mom!"

"What? Are you nuts? This little sleazeball was nothing but trouble. I'm lucky I'm not expelled."

"No, if Nose hadn't gotten loose, then Officer Copper wouldn't have come to school and found out about that Ed Stickwell guy. Nose got it all started. I can't wait to call my mom. She's going to be so happy that no one thinks she's a thief anymore."

"Will they let her come back to work today?"

"Probably not today, but hopefully tomorrow."

"Crystal, where were you hiding when you first ran downstairs?"

"Behind the barrel of cans. I can't believe you didn't see me. I saw you. If I wasn't so scared, I would have laughed when you adjusted that purple sock – oh, I almost forgot – I think my hair ribbon is still down there."

I wait for her as she skips back down the stairs toward a splotch of bright green in the corner.

"Roland? Is that your grandma's voice I hear?"

"Oh, no! We'd better hurry!"

When we get to the first floor, everything is back to normal, except that Mom is standing in the hallway. The thick blue towel that usually covers our back seat is wrapped around her waist and she's arguing real loud with Grandma, who's still sitting in the chair I put outside the lunchroom door.

"He's *not* having an insulin reaction, Zinnia," Grandma shouts. "Taking Iris has *nothing* to do with diabetes!"

"He's either lost his mind or he's hypoglycemic, Mother. Are you *sure* he injected the right..."

"Mom, I'm fine," I say, rushing over to them. "Grandma, I told you I'd bring Iris back. And look who else I've got." I jiggle Nose and give him a big squeeze.

"See, Zinnia? I knew he'd catch the little beast." And then turning to me, she hollers even louder, "My new purple sock had better not be damaged, young man! I'll never find another pair that matches my hat *and* my gloves."

"Grandma, shhh, are you trying to make me get detention? We have to be quiet in the halls, remember?"

I set Iris gently down on Grandma's lap while Nose tries to wiggle free of my arms to lick her face – and her pizza-stained plate. I glance back toward the stairs where Crystal is fussing with her hair, trying to fasten the ribbon without the aid of a mirror. I finally catch her eye and nod for her to come over. She smiles and shrugs, as if to say, 'Sure, why not?'

"Mom, Grandma, this is Crystal Nellson. She helped catch Nose."

Crystal smiles and says, "Hi. He sure makes a lot of noise for such a little fella."

"Yes, he certainly does," agrees Mom, her eyes shifting slowly between Crystal and me. "I'm afraid his adventures at school this morning are all my fault. I should have never opened my window. And I want you to know, Crystal, that I don't usually wear a big blue towel out in public. That naughty little dog spilled tea all over my pants."

"It's a cute towel, though," Crystal says, giggling. "Very stylish. And it matches our school colors perfectly."

Mom flashes her a grateful smile. "You can borrow it some time," she says, worry returning to her face when she turns back to me. "Are you ready to go back to class, son?"

"No, I need my book bag. Is it still outside on the bus ramp?"

"Not anymore. I didn't want it to get wet in all that melting snow so I put it in the van... What is that terrible smell?"

"It might be yesterday's lunch on my clothes, or maybe the boiler room door is still open. What happened to our pizza plan, Grandma? Couldn't you hold onto Nose?"

"He snatched the pizza and ran away. Never even slowed down. If this chair had wheels I would have caught him myself."

Mom shakes her head, disgusted. "When Little Bradley," she glances at Crystal, "I mean, when Officer Copper and his dog-catching pole showed up, I had to drive across the street to the library to find a legal place to park. By the time I put on my towel and ran back to find out what was going on, Nose had all but disappeared. I hope you don't get suspended because of this, Roland. We can't keep having..."

She pauses and looks at Crystal again. "Did I hear correctly? Your last name is Nellson? You're Opal and Mel's daughter?"

Crystal nods and grins, wiggling her eyebrows suggestively at Grandma. "And yes, that means Alfred Rodriguez is my grandpa."

"Did you say Alfred Rodriguez?" shouts Grandma, looking up from her leg adjustments.

"Shhh, yes, and Crystal knows all about what Nose did to his rasp..."

"We're very sorry about that," interrupts Mom, adjusting her towel sheepishly. "I hope the new plants will be all right."

Crystal shrugs. "My grandpa won't know until next spring. But we don't care. I mean, your dog is sooo funny. And I'm sooo glad he showed up here at school today."

Mom gives me an odd look and then follows her investigative instincts. "What seems funny to *me*, is that you're not in class right now, Crystal..."

Crystal looks surprised and glances at me for help. I don't think she wants me blabbing about her mom's troubles, so I don't have much to say. I give it a try anyway.

"Yeah, well – um – okay, Crystal had to go down in the basement for something and then after I went down, too, Nose must have followed. We managed to catch him in the boiler room where they have this giant trash compactor. And Mom? You'll be happy to know that I stopped him from getting into all that garbage."

She studies me and nods her head slowly. "It sounds like there's a few missing details to this story, especially the parts about why you took your grandmother's leg, but I guess I can wait until after school to hear the rest. You two had better get back to class."

"And you'd better get Nose out of here," I say. "The next bell's going to ring any minute."

"Oh, no! We can't go through that again! Mother, are you ready to go?"

Nose tries to squirm out of my arms when he hears his favorite words, but there's no way I'll let him escape again.

"Yes, dear, I'm all set. Iris is secured and back in service," Grandma says cheerfully as she stands up, adjusts her huge purple hat, and leans on her three-legged cane.

"It was nice to meet you, Crystal. Say hello to your grandfather for me. Now be a honey, Roland, and grab my purse. You can get your books when you carry it and Nose out to the van."

"Okay, I'll be right there."

I sling Grandma's hideous pink and green bag over my shoulder and wait for Mom and Grandma to leave. Then I sneak a smile at Crystal.

"I guess you don't need my help anymore, but I still have your mom's printouts in my book bag. Should I give them to you in front of the locker room after school like we planned?"

"Yep, but take your time. I have basketball practice and you have to stay after school today, too."

"Why? Do I have detention already?"

"No, didn't you hear the announcements this morning? You have a meeting with the cheerleaders. Congratulations, Roland. You're a mascot. You got picked as an Abominable Snowperson."

"Me? You mean, I got picked for something? I'm abominable?"

But before she can answer, a loud melody buzzes like an electronic alarm in the hallway behind us, "Lavender blue, dilly dilly…"

Crystal and I look at each other and laugh.

"What can I say, Crystal? With a family like mine, I'm a perfect choice. For being *abominable*, that is. For being really, really, REALLY abominable!"

How abominable does Roland get?
Find out by reading Nose 'n Me Mystery #2:
The ABOMINABLE Abominable Snowperson
AKA: The Case of the Dogged Delinquent

Facts You Should Know About Juvenile Diabetes

- Juvenile Diabetes is also called Type I Diabetes.
- More than one million Americans have it.
- 35 children in America are diagnosed every day. Some of them are babies.
- Grown-ups get juvenile diabetes, too.
- It is not caused by being overweight or eating too much sugar.
- A person with juvenile diabetes has to inject insulin because his pancreas has stopped making it. Insulin is needed to convert sugary foods to energy. We need insulin to stay alive.
- Type I diabetes is much less common than Type II diabetes. In this book, Roland has Type I diabetes and his grandma has Type II diabetes. They can both be difficult to manage. If left untreated, both types cause serious damage to many parts of the body.
- There is no cure for juvenile diabetes, but scientists are working every day to find one.
- The Juvenile Diabetes Research Foundation (JDRF) was formed in 1970 in order to raise money to find a cure.

What Can You Do To Help?

Every fall, JDRF holds its biggest fund-raiser, the Walk to Cure Diabetes, in over 225 cities worldwide. By walking to cure diabetes, you can help raise money to pay for expensive laboratories, equipment, and researchers, all needed to find a cure. Some kids form school teams, and others just participate on their own. You can find out what to do by contacting JDRF at:

Juvenile Diabetes Research Foundation
120 Wall Street
New York, NY 10005-4001
Telephone 1-800-533-2873
Web Site: www.jdrf.org

Do You Want To Help Even More?

Write to your United States Senator and Representative. Ask them to help find a cure, too! That's called, being an advocate. When we understand and accept kids like Roland, being an advocate is easy to do. He believes that a cure is possible. Advocates can make it happen!

Facts You Should Know About Beagles

- Beagles are classified as hounds.
- They are usually black on the back, white on the legs, belly, and chest, and tan around the face and sides. This type of coloring is called tricolor. Freckles and other spots are common, too.
- Beagles can be red and white or yellow and white, too.
- Snoopy is a famous cartoon beagle.
- Beagles were first bred to be scent hounds that worked together in a pack. They have a highly developed sense of smell, which enables them to follow foxes and rabbits for long distances throughout the countryside.
- Some airports use beagles to smell luggage for illegal drugs or foreign foods that may be infested with undesirable insects.
- Beagles bay loudly when they catch the scent of something, allowing hunters to easily find them.
- Some beagles are difficult to train because they have strong instincts to be independent, energetic, and very stubborn.
- They come in two sizes: short (15 inches tall) or shorter (13 inches tall).
- Most beagles love kids, but sometimes they lick too much and play too energetically.
- Because beagles are pack animals, they usually get along with other pets. They are rarely mean, but can often be disobedient.
- They were first introduced to America in 1876. Before that, they mostly lived in England, Ireland, and Wales.
- People should not bring a beagle into their homes unless they are willing to provide regular exercise. Beagles have loads of energy and don't like being cooped up.
- Beagles are often fat because their extremely well developed sense of smell never fails to locate food.

Interested in learning more about beagles? Try typing BEAGLE into a search engine on the internet. You'll be amazed!

Is this a four-legged opera singer or a furry smoke-detector?
WooWooWoo knows?

About the author

Christine Petrell Kallevig has been a professional storyteller and published author since 1991. Many of her books combine origami with stories, a technique she calls, "Storigami." She makes frequent visits to schools and libraries nationwide, telling stories and folding paper. When she's home in Ohio, she spends most of her time chasing her rambunctious beagle, Kirby, who's only slightly better behaved than Roland's dog, Nose. During the rare moments when Kirby is quiet and not trying to escape into the woods behind her house, Christine invents new storigami stories and writes middle-grade fiction.

Readers can send E-mail to her at foldalong@att.net or write to:
P. O. Box 470505, Cleveland, OH 44147-0505

Purchase extra copies of this book, *Please Pass Grandma's Leg* (**ISBN 0-9628769-3-3 $9.95**) or any of these other books by Christine Petrell Kallevig at your favorite bookstore, or use the form on the next page to order directly from the publisher.

The *ABOMINABLE* Abominable Snowperson AKA: The Case of the Dogged Delinquent - Trouble rules as Roland and Nose attend obedience school and they both become suspiciously famous. But not in a good way. Not in a good way at all... Available September, 2004. **ISBN 0-9628769-2-5 $9.95**

Carry Me Home Cuyahoga - Dramatic historical fiction set in Cleveland, Ohio in 1806. It tells the true story of how Ben, a fugitive slave, was rescued from Lake Erie and nursed back to health by the dynamic Carter family. Recommended for grades 3 and up. Paperback. 105 pages. **ISBN 0-9628769-7-6 $9.95**

Fold-Along Stories: Quick & Easy Origami Tales For Beginners - 12 very short stories are illustrated by the progressive folds of 12 very easy origami models. Complete illustrated folding directions are next to the stories for carefree use by all ages. Paperback. 80 pages. **ISBN 0-9628769-9-2 $11.50**

Holiday Folding Stories: Storytelling & Origami Together For Holiday Fun - 9 original stories are combined with the progressive folding steps of 9 origami models. Includes Columbus Day, Halloween, Thanksgiving, Hanukkah, Christmas, Valentine's Day, Easter, May Day, and Mother's Day. Ages 4-adult. Paperback. 96 pages. **ISBN 0-9628769-1-7 $11.50**

Bible Folding Stories: Old Testament Stories & Paperfolding Together As One - Includes The 23rd Psalm, Jacob's ladder, Jonah's big fish, Noah's dove, Moses' basket, Ruth & Naomi's spike of wheat, Joseph's robe, Elijah's jar of oil, and Sarah's baby. Recommended for all ages and all Judeo-Christian faiths. Paperback. 96 pages. **ISBN 0-9628769-4-1 $11.50**

All About Pockets: Storytime Activities for Early Childhood - The ultimate guide for how to use pockets to achieve educational and social goals in early childhood classrooms. Paperback. 128 pages. **ISBN 0-9628769-6-8 $9.95**

Library patrons: please photocopy

Name:_____

Address:_____

_____

City/State:_____

Zip Code:_____

Please send me:

Qty.	ISBN number or book title	Price	Total
	SUBTOTAL		
	OH residents add 7% sales tax		
	Postage & Handling: Add $2 (1st book) $1 @ additional book		
	US Dollars only TOTAL ENCLOSED		

Write checks to: Storytime Ink International
Mail to: Storytime Ink International
P. O. Box 470505
Cleveland, OH 44147-0505

Allow 2 weeks for delivery. Questions? Call 440-838-4881
or E-Mail at storytimeink@att.net